PO.

Jamie Glaser

All proceeds go to St. Louis County SAVE

Poppy is a work of fiction. Any similarity to persons living or deceased is purely coincidental.

Poppy © Jamie Glaser 2024

ISBN: 9798882775468
Independently published

Edited by Debbie Manber Kupfer

All proceeds go to St. Louis County SAVE

Dedication

Poppy is dedicated to dogs everywhere and to the people who love and advocate for them.

ABOUT THE CHARITY

Thank you for purchasing *Poppy*. All money raised from sales of this book will be donated to St. Louis County SAVE.

St. Louis County SAVE is a 501c(3) non-profit whose mission is to improve the quality of life for animals in STL County and lower the euthanasia rate to as close to zero as possible.

Their primary objectives are to:

1. Ensure that the welfare of the animals and the community is always the FIRST priority in all decisions made regarding the animals of St. Louis County.

2. Advocate for animals in the St. Louis County.

3. Increase awareness of St. Louis County residents about issues with the shelter and mobilize them to get involved.

4. Educate policy makers about issues and encourage them to take a proactive approach to resolving them.

To learn more about them or make a donation visit their website at stlcsave.weebly.com

Chapter One

Patricia

Patricia Rueben clipped the last of her rose bushes, shortening them for the upcoming autumn season. It was Sunday, the only day she didn't have a commitment, and incidentally, her least favorite day of the week. Sunday was supposed to be "funday" as all of her friends on Facebook expressed, posting pictures of their children, grandchildren, and pets at various places around Denver and beyond. She supposed she could post Sunday pictures to her account as well, but it was difficult to get a selfie in while being berated by one's husband for one thing or another.

She sighed as she heard his hummer pull up the driveway. As always, whenever he drove up to the house their neighbor's corgi, Skylar barked incessantly. She hated her husband. Patricia understood Skylar's sentiment. She married Sebastian in June of 2001. He didn't want to get married because he didn't like titles, but at that time he claimed he loved her. So they were married and the honeymoon stage ended even before the honeymoon began. Patricia knew he was a harsh and arrogant man, but at that time, she found his no nonsense ways sexy and almost charming. She was such a free spirit herself, and to be with such a successful and wealthy man who acquired anything he put his mind to was appealing to her. She hoped he would bring balance to her life. In her thirties and in her naiveté she yearned for someone to "complete her." She was always told that her head was in the clouds and that she needed someone to bring her down to earth. Sebastian Garrett was just the person who would tame the free spirit in her, and at fifty-five she felt that he had. And she had lost the best part of herself. She fondled the large turquoise stone necklace around her neck. Its beads were round but not perfectly so. Random edges jutted out, cold and smooth to her touch. She had purchased them on one of the few trips that she had taken away from Sebastian during the twenty-two years of her marriage. She had taken a road trip to New Mexico with her friend Pamela and she had purchased them from a Zuni Indian who was selling them on the streets. She said the beads would bring good luck, and while that was untrue, throughout the years they had brought her hope. They had reminded her of who she once was and who she wanted to be again. A woman who purchases from street vendors. A woman who encourages small business owners with her finances and her words. A woman unafraid to be her true self. But at the moment she felt none of these things. She felt like she was a puppet and Sebastian held the string. All she could do was the dance he instructed her because she felt some days that even her limbs were not her own.

He came in grumbling as usual. "The beds are not made, the floor isn't swept, there's shit everywhere, and where is she? Out playing with the damn flowers. As usual. She works thirty hours a week, I'm in the office at least sixty, but does she do *anything* in the house? No. Of course not. Because that would require lifting a finger to something besides typing away on other people's manuscripts. Never mind, I'll do it." He stomped up the stairs, threw the comforter off of the unmade bed and began straightening the sheets. Patricia snorted laughter as she looked at the clock. 5:06 p.m. Why was he making a bed he was going to unmake in four hours?

Patricia was hurt by the way her husband treated her but she was not afraid of him. She could hold her own to his hurling of insults but what terrified her the most was that her life was passing her by as she endured his tyranny and pretended to be happily married to those who asked her how she was.

Sebastian was a very successful stock broker. He made enough to pay for every house in their old money neighborhood, and while that was a slight exaggeration, he could retire at age 56 and never have to work another day in his life. However Sebastian loved one thing in his life. His job, and leaving that job would require him to look at his wife as opposed to barking commands at her as he left for the office every morning, sometimes even on weekends. This Sunday, at 5 p.m., he had come back from the office, which he had left for at 7:30 that morning. She knew he didn't really have much to do there that would require him to be in the office on a Sunday. He could work from home most days if he so desired, but instead took the five mile commute each morning in his enormous Hummer, at least ten miles over the speed limit, practically running over kids on bikes, as well as drivers going the legal limit. While spending her weekends alone was sad, there was also a sense of relief that he was gone.

On Monday morning Patricia was getting ready to teach a class at her friend's yoga studio. It has always been a dream of hers to own her own studio, as she had been studying yoga since she was in high school. She'd had so many dreams before marrying Sebastian.

Patricia was brought up in a reformed Jewish household, where it seemed her mother's religious beliefs spanned to "young ladies were supposed to go off and get married." Much to her mother's chagrin Patricia was still single at age 32; though she and Sebastian had been on again, off again for four years by that time.

Patricia's parents couldn't stand Sebastian. He was rude, he was never on time, and he argued with everyone over everything. Though it was hard to prove, some of the comments he made could be construed as anti-Semitic. But he was hard working, had a lot of money, and at the time Patricia was crazy about him. He would whisk her away for the weekend to these romantic places, off the map, small, intimate and she admitted, despite his brash and abrasive ways sometimes, she always had a wonderful time. She loved trying new things and he brought that part out in her, encouraging her to try new foods and travel to new places. He took her to Boulder and she fell in love with everything about its culture, but when she asked if they could move there he said there was no way because his job was located in Denver and he would never leave his job. She understood and until they were married they visited it often. In those early days, while he still had his moods and moments when he was condescending to her and devalued her, they traveled so much and had such a wonderful time that she chose to overlook what everyone else saw as obvious. Sebastian Garrett could put on a good show, but like a stray dog in your basement, he couldn't hide his true colors forever.

Now twenty three years later his colors bled out more often. Her friend Pamela, who was a Licensed Professional Counselor and had studied psychology all of her life, theorized that the older one gets the harder it becomes to put on a show for the world. Sebastian had a hard time convincing the world that he was a mensch twenty years ago, and these days, the neighbors began to notice.

As she was grabbing her keys, she heard a pounding on her door. Sebastian had left for the office two hours ago, so she went to answer it. It was her neighbor, Jack Bordon. He did not look happy.

"Is Sebastian home?"

"No, I'm sorry, he's not. He left for work a few hours ago."

"When he gets home, you tell him that if he *ever* tries to run my daughter Jenna over on her scooter again, I will grab his nuts so hard he'll be squeaking for a week. And when I'm done I will sue his ass for attempting to run over a nine-year-old girl. Have a nice day." And with that, Jack slammed *her* door in her face, before storming down the front walkway.

Oh boy, she thought. She knew that Jack was overreacting but not by much. While Sebastian would never attempt manslaughter, especially on a child, his patience was thin as gossamer and she knew he probably dodged around her as she scooted over Brisbane Ave which had no sidewalk. He used his Hummer like a weapon and he knew it as well as she did. But he would never admit it and now their neighbor wanted to kill him. Part of her, the vindictive part, wished that Jack would make good on his promise. Watching that SOB limp for a week wouldn't be the worst thing ever.

After yoga she got a text from Sebastian. "Make yourself useful and pick up some razors on the way home." No thank you, no specification of how many or what brand though she knew the brand he usually bought. She drove to Walmart and when she pulled into the parking space, she saw a gray figure running around the parking lot. There was some slush on the ground as it had recently snowed. Upon a closer look, she saw that it was a dog—medium, gray and terrified—dodging vehicles here and there trying to find a corner to cower into. She loved dogs but she knew getting involved would cause more trouble than she was ready for from Sebastian. As one would guess, he hated dogs.

Poppy

I don't know how I ended up here, hungry and alone, I have very few things I am afraid of. I have to be brave or I'll run away from potential food. However there is one thing I'm terrified of. The moving boxes with the wheels. A beast with a domain would growl howl and yap at those things like crazy, but me? Out here, on my own, an orphan, all I can do is cower. Not so hard to do when there's one of 'em or even two but put a million of 'em in a small space with humans walking around, all smelling different, the big wheeled boxes blowing black stuff all over the place. Well, it's enough to knock someone off their haunches. Never mind what color they turn the snow. And they say yellow snow is a bad color....

Let me rewind. I live alone. Which if that meant that I was the queen of my very own castle and I decided who to let in, would be a great thing, but I live on the streets. The streets are hard and scary but there are some nice people. The guy who sells sausage always leaves the leftover ones out for me and a bunch of hissy scraggly pissers who fight me for them. I'm not afraid of them, but they see me and run away like they surely should. Little brats! Sausage is for the dogs.

I'm not surprised the dumb ole hissy things don't like me. They're jealous because they're not a dog and a lesser species. However, humans? Some are nice, but some want to kill me. One good thing about the ratty hissers. They don't have scary metal things in their hands when they're mad. Just claws which aren't that impressive if you ask me. But a frightened and angry human? Well, let me backtrack a little bit.

I have no idea how long I've been alone. My earliest memories are warm and furry and full of milk. Two brothers, one sister, and a nice furry mama. It was cold and snowy a lot but it was warm with her. My siblings were greedy and always tried to take all the milk, but at least I wasn't homeless and got food on a regular basis. Mama lived under a porch where these nice humans lived. They'd never let her inside but at least they didn't shoo her out when they saw she had babies. Then one day those people left. These guys came, they had poles and mama got scared. At that point we were getting bigger and could eat solid food. Would have been nice if there was any out there, but the only thing we were facing was what mama called incarceration. I don't know what that word means, but it's the last thing she said to us before she ran off. She ran one way, and as the people with the poles and cages went after me I ran another. I don't know where these people wanted to take me, but they weren't getting their paws on me! Kind of a dumb move on my part to run because for as long as I can remember after that day I've been scrounging for food, oftentimes unsuccessfully.

Not eating is one of the worst things a dog can imagine unless they're faced with the scary metal thing. I was walking around one day and suddenly I smelled something. A lot of things. Basil. Tomatoes. Pork! Beef! My mouth started to water so much I began drooling like a Dane. How embarrassing, but can ya blame me? I mean beef and pork married into a medley of spices? Was today my lucky day? No. No it was not. I reached the big metal round thing where the smell was coming from. It was closed. Darn.

I'm not nocturnal by nature but an opportunist I am. Sometimes I'd stay awake at night to observe the big tailed creatures with the little masks forage. These creatures smelled like they would taste nice but at the same time they looked like someone you don't want to mess with. But at least I could be a silent student in their night class in food finding. The little creature would use their paw to lift the lid of this round metal thing. They made it look so easy, but looking down at my flat clumsy paws I wasn't sure I could pull it off. However, tonight was as good a time as any to try. I climbed up to the metal circle and wouldn't you know, my big ole body knocked it down, rattling as it fell. Darn. That was loud. Just then the door opened and I heard a human. They didn't sound happy. At all.

"Ellen, call the pound, one of those goddamn strays is nosing through the trashcan again!" I wasn't a hundred percent sure of what this human was saying but his voice sounded commanding. I figured he'd boss around the fellow human in his company and go back into his shelter, leaving me a few more minutes for round two with this very stubborn yet very aromatic container. Wrong. He approached me slowly and stealthily, unlike the last oafs that pursued me, tripping over their own paws. I looked up. He had something in his hand, silver and shiny and he was aiming it at me.

Then I smelled something, something even stronger than beef. Fear. Being a stray and not having much experience with humans I had no idea how they would react to fear. I took a step back, and just then the female human approached. Then she did something I never thought one would do. She screamed. "Ed!! It's a pit bull. Get the gun!"

"I have the gun you dumbass. I'm afraid it's going to kill me if I don't kill it. He backed up a few more feet and began to move the shiny thing. There was a loud noise and something told me to run as fast as I could, balls of beef be damned for now!

I ran until I was out of breath. I was still hungry and disappointed not to mention reeling from the panic I had just felt, but more than anything I was confused. The only other encounter I'd had with humans was with the fools with the cages who thought they could outrun me. And while they failed miserably, they seemed very assured of themselves, and I smelled confidence. I've never smelled fear before and for some reason it was the most threatening and foreboding sensation I had ever encountered. Scared? Of what? Protective of their beef maybe but why afraid? Being practically a puppy and with a limited self-awareness I couldn't imagine how I looked, but the man with the scary thing in his hand had to be bigger than me. Even the female next to him was. What on earth did I represent to them that would cause fear?

I had very little time to ponder this as I still hadn't eaten and I was going on day two. Thankfully, the white cold stuff doubled as water so I never went thirsty. But water ain't bacon and I needed to find some, or something of the likes. Soon.

That's how I ended up here in this place that smelled like fried chicken and looked like the motor raceway. There were very few humans walking outside but I spotted one. I sniffed. Female, about eight years old in dog years. She had a good vibe. But best of all she was going into the place that smelled like chicken. So I did my best to turn on my charm though my social skills were lacking for lack of human interaction.

"Excuse me." I whimpered. "I just happened to notice that you were going into that building. I highly doubt my species is allowed in such an establishment so if you wouldn't mind picking up a drumstick or two and just setting it in front of me, it would be much obliged. Please?" The human looked down at me and smiled. I smelled worry, but at least not the fear I smelled from the people with the scary metal thing. She started to bark and though I wasn't sure what she was saying it wasn't said maliciously.

"Hi honey. You're cute but if I bought a dog home along with the razors my husband would kill us both. You're probably better off with someone else but if you're still here when I come back, I'll think about it." And with that she walked inside the moving double door.

Patricia

Patricia shook her head. Poor little thing. If she weren't constantly in the proverbial doghouse herself with her cantankerous husband, she'd take the little dog home in a heartbeat. She loved dogs, but of course he didn't because that would imply that he had a soul. She hoped and prayed the little dog would be gone by the time she came back outside but bought a bag of beef jerky at the checkout just in case.

When she exited Walmart, she saw the dog in the exact same place she had left her looking terrified, yet still expectant that someone would feed her or better yet bring her home. She sat down on a bench and the timid little creature came up to her, and sniffed her bag. She took out the package of beef jerky and tore open the top.

Poppy

It was that human again. I sniffed the bag in her lap. No chicken but something smelled good! Dry. Smoky. She put a piece in front of me. I devoured it and another piece. Whatever this was sure bit back but my canines were in tip top shape being practically a puppy. I ate and ate until she barked again in her language.

"Well, girl, that's the last of it. Gee I wish I could take you home but...."

After the last word she uttered something changed in her demeanor. I know humans don't normally growl but her face hardened. Her eyes narrowed and her posture stiffened. I sniffed and while I smelled a hint of fear, there was something else I smelled. Anger. She seemed like she was an animal whose territory was being threatened.. Defensive! That was it. This middle-aged female was feeling territorial. Over what I didn't know. I just wish she had another bag of that smoky stuff.

Patricia

Patricia had had it. She looked at the little dog, thin, afraid and obviously homeless. She was frustrated that nobody did anything about it or the myriad of other homeless animals in Denver and beyond, but more so about the fact that she had the resources to care for this dog but Mr. King of the Castle Dictator forbade it. She sighed. She'd take the little dog to the local Humane Society to at least get her off the streets. She wasn't sure if the dog would follow her as she was out of jerky but she walked and made a hand motion to come on and the dog followed, slowly, head down, but willingly. At least she could do something for her.

There comes a pivotal moment in our lives when we come to realize we've been living a life that doesn't fit. We swallow and put on a show for the world, shrouded in wealth and aptitude, hiding our true selves. We change our name and our clothes to blend in, because standing out and being our true authentic self is terrifying. And it's not worth the risk. Until one day, it is.

As Patricia drove past the Humane Society she debated bringing the dog in there. While she seemed sweet enough she knew that the shelters were teeming with cats and dogs and that a common little pit bull would be lost among the many many needy animals that came through. Instead of going into the building, she pulled into a shopping center and called them.

"Humane Society, this is Andy, how may I help you?"

"Andy, hello. I found a little female pit bull in the Walmart parking lot and I was thinking of bringing her to you, and I want an honest answer. What are the odds of her finding a good home? She seems young and healthy albeit a little thin. Very skittish but hungry, so motivated by food. I wish I had more to give you but we met fifteen minutes ago, so…"

"Well, she sounds cute! I'm not going to lie, mam, we have a lot of pit bulls. All wonderful dogs but unfortunately people aren't lining up at the door to adopt them. We work with some wonderful rescues. But I'm not going to sugarcoat it, of all the 150 dogs we have for adoption over here at least a hundred are pit bulls. If there's any way you can keep her or try to reunite her with her owner that would be the best for her."

"Do you scan microchips?"

"Absolutely! Bring her in and maybe by some miracle she has a family out there."

Patricia looked at the little dog. If she did have a family they were pretty shitty people because their dog was practically emaciated, but just to prove herself wrong she took her to get scanned.

Poppy

I looked out the window. Oh damn. This wasn't good. I knew that chewy snack was too good to be true. It was a trick. She was taking me to the clowns with the catch poles to be manhandled and thrown in a cage. I began to bark. Loud. Maybe if I was loud enough she would get tired of the barking and turn me loose."

"Shh, it's ok, girl. We're just going to see if you belong to someone, before I unleash hell's fury and bring you home."

Patricia

She led the dog into the building, but since she didn't have a leash or any more enticing snacks, this was difficult. She finally lifted her up. Ugh, she didn't exactly smell like roses, Sebastian would just love a smelly dog in the house. An employee opened the door and smiled. "Hi, I'm Andy. I think we spoke on the phone?"

"What tipped you off?" Patricia smiled.

"She sure is cute, but thin. Come on little lady, we're going to see if you belong to someone."

Poppy

For a place with a few hundred dogs it sure did smell astringent. I sniffed the male human we were following. No fear, seemed docile enough and he didn't have a catch pole. He wasn't erratic and oafish like the dummies who went after me, but I sure didn't like the idea of being in this building. I had a feeling some of the dogs who entered never made it out.

First they waved a wand over me and the big male human shook his head. Then they made me stand on a cold metal square. I refused, but the female threw some more of that smoky stuff onto it so I went up to eat it and they seemed satisfied after that. As we walked back to the door I saw all of these small rooms with dogs just like me behind them. Some were chewing toys, some were howling, and others were just sitting there, looking sad. I didn't want to be like them, even if I was given food every day.

Patricia

"I want to take her home, I really do." Patricia told Andy. "I just have this husband at home, and well, you don't need to know my drama, but he'll have a cow, I know it. He really doesn't like dogs. In fact, the dog next door hates him. I almost hate to say this but this little girl is probably better off in a cage, at least she'll be fed."

Andy shook his head. "I have to respectfully disagree. This little pup seems sweet but little gray gals like her are a dime a dozen around here. The likelihood of her being noticed and snatched up is slim. We never want to euthanize for space. Ever. But there have been times when that has been our only option. I don't know if I believe in serendipity or not but this dog found you. Mam, I'm imploring you. Take her home. If it doesn't work out, you know where we're located but it's worth a shot."

She smiled, tiredly. "Thank you, Andy. It's hard to argue with that. She grabbed the leash that he had given her to walk her around the shelter. Come on, missy. We can at least hide you for a night!"

Poppy

So we were back in the moving box again. I had to admit I hated these things a little less when I was in them. It was warm and soft and the human was such welcome company though she was as tense as a tough piece of meat. She stopped the box and opened the door. I jumped out, and immediately the dog next door started yapping a mile a minute. I cocked my ears to try to understand what she was carrying on about.

"No, no, no, no, no! Don't go in the house! The missus is nice enough but the male is as crabby as a tabby! He hates dogs! Save your hide and RUN!"

I sighed and looked at the female human. She was the first of her species who has offered me food in days and she didn't have a scary metal thing in her hand. If there was more food in there I was going to take my chances.

"I appreciate the warning and all, but your pampered little tail doesn't know what it's like to be a stray so I think I'm going to go in there and see what I can get my mouth on."

"Well good luck with *that*," she huffed. "Just don't complain to *me* if he kicks your can to the curb."

"Thanks for the warning." I assured her using my best big sister bark. She proceeded to bark incessantly. Little dogs sure were a different breed!

She led me up a few stony steps into a wide open space. *Wow, I thought, nice shelter.* I heard the sound of boots on the ground and looked up. If this was the male that little Corgi was yapping about maybe I should have taken her more seriously. This guy smelled like bad news. I sniffed again. Fear. Ah, but a scaredy-cat eh? I sniffed again. The fear smell wasn't coming from him. I looked up at the female. It was coming from her. I stood protectively in front of her though I had no idea what that would do, if anything. Some things are just instinctual.

"Patricia, what is this?"

"What the hell does it look like?" She tossed a package to him. "Here are the razors."

"Dirty mutt wasn't on the shopping list, Patricia. Where did you find it?"

Dirty mutt? It? This was getting personal!

"I found *her* in the parking lot. What the hell was I supposed to do, leave her there? She was starving! "

"Take her to a shelter?"

"I did, they weighed and scanned her for a chip and she had none. The guy at the front desk told me they're so full there and her likelihood of being adopted was so small and I just couldn't leave her there! Sebastian, we have so much space. My God, if we just reserved a room just for her, at least for a few weeks, and I'll post online her availability to a good home, at least she'd be safe for the time being."

"*Of course* 'the guy at the front desk told you to keep her!' Those people are lazy. Probably makes ten bucks an hour. He doesn't want to do his job."

"For your information *Andrew* wanted me to keep her because he actually cares about these animals. But on their website it said they have about ninety adoptable dogs and quite a few of them look like her, probably from similar situations."

"Patricia, every time you get one of these stupid *whims* of yours I end up paying for it. I'm sick of it. If you keep that dog I'm divorcing you, I've had it."

I didn't know what this dumb ole human was saying but when he finished his last sentence all of the fear smell vanished from the female. I looked up and her jaw was set firm and her eyes were narrow. She looked like she was ready to defend something.

Patricia

"You know what, Sebastian. I'm not even going to try to fight you. I'm not going to negotiate with you, or apologize again like I've been doing for the past twenty five years. You keep your ridiculously enormous house. I'd rather live under a porch than here with you and your big mouth. You disgust me with your tyranny. Maybe this dog was a sign from God that I need to move on. Maybe she was sent here to stroke your inferno of a temper so I could see your true shit colors. And by the way, Jack from next door came over this morning and said that if you ever try to run his daughter over again, he'll whack your dick off or something like that. Have a good night."

"Where are you going?"

"Anywhere but here."

Sometimes we have to take a stand, even when our knees are wobbly. It takes wiping away the blindness we chose to live with in order to see a situation with clarity. It takes remembering our name, the one given before we gave our name away. We know ourselves from the inside out, and as we journey through life, we either find more of ourselves or lose more, depending on the company we keep. Sometimes we have to let go of the security we knew to embrace the freedom we always longed for.

Patricia sat in her Jeep, shaking from her confrontation with Sebastian that had been bubbling on the surface for years. She looked at the little pup at her side and patted her head. "Thank you, girl." She realized it was the first time that she had actually touched the animal with the exception of leashing her. She had distanced herself from this animal's plight, a cocoon around her emotions just in case she couldn't find the courage to stand her ground against her husband. Feeling the coarse warm fur beneath her palm, Patricia broke down. She sobbed and sobbed, mourning simultaneously the many years she had held herself captive to the endeavor of pleasing an impossible person, as well as the unknown plight of this little dog. She had always loved animals and in the middle of her marriage she had swallowed so many of her own desires in order to fit the life he wanted for them.

Once she composed herself and dried her eyes she looked over at the dog. She had read somewhere that dogs don't always like their personal space invaded,(or was that cats?) and to be respectful of their space. But at the same time this animal had probably never felt the touch of a human before. So she took her chances and wrapped her arms around the dog's thick neck. She didn't move, just grunted softly and settled down deeply into the soft front seat of her Jeep. Patricia put her cheek up against the coarse warm fur and once again began sobbing.

"Thank you, girl. For being right where you needed to be this afternoon. You'll never understand, but you saved us both."

Poppy

The human was wrong. In that moment, in my own way, as I felt her warm tears against me, I understood perfectly.

Patricia

Patricia had many friends but she had abandoned the majority of them over the past years because he didn't like them. He called them fembots and said they were a bad influence. Thankfully she still taught yoga with Pamela and had her contact information available.

"Hey, what's up?"

"So, I did something."

"You left Mr. Perfect?"

"Not exactly. So I was at Walmart getting razors because he requested. I saw this little gray dog."

"Aww."

"Yes, she was really cute, and clearly hungry. I bought her some beef jerky and took her to the Humane Society to be scanned in case she had a microchip. Unfortunately she did not. I asked the guy if she had a chance of getting adopted. He answered that while she's really cute they have so many dogs, especially pit bull types that she would be much better off in a home. Of course. So knowing he would blow a gasket I took the dog home."

"He blew one?"

"He did but so did I. This is the last straw, Pamela. We have five bedrooms. Could we NOT keep the poor thing in one room, find her a permanent home, and when she's done with the room, clean it out? Better Life comes once a month to clean the house. But of course, no, because it would inconvenience his life. In the middle of me begging him, I realized I felt more like his child than his wife. And I've felt that way for years. It took this little dog to solidify this. Anyway, now both of us are homeless."

"No you're not, come on over. I love ya, Patricia, but even if I didn't you have a *dog* in your car! Bring it on over!"

She looked at the dog as she turned the key to the engine. "I burned a lot of bridges being married to that selfish old tomcat back there, but tonight we're going to meet the one bridge I haven't burned. If it weren't for her we'd both be homeless. Or in a nice hotel that allows pets, but this is much more personal."

"Oh my *goodness*!" Pamela ran out to the car. "What a cutie you found! Much cuter than that old husband of yours!"

"Agree. If it wasn't for her I'd be home now, doing his bidding. I really think this is a sign that I need to take a stand. I have no idea what I'm going to do with this dog, but step one was realizing that I can't share a home with a man who won't share a home with a dog for even a short time while we find her a home. He wouldn't even have to look at her. She could have stayed in the finished basement."

"And ruin his man cave? How could you suggest that?"

"I'm inconsiderate." Patricia rolled her eyes as the dog bounded out of the car.

"Oh, shit, I need to grab the leash!"

They took her into Pamela's two-story condo and sat on the couch.

"Here, try this new flavor of Pam's Pops. It's salted caramel and cinnamon."

Pamela ran two businesses, a yoga studio as well as a popcorn company.

"Oh, it's delicious! And I haven't had dinner yet."

"Here." She handed Patricia a bag. "So, do you have a name for this little lady yet?"

Just then Pamela dropped a piece of popcorn and the dog snatched it up. Both ladies laughed.

"Poppy?" Pamela suggested.

"I like it!"

The dog barked. She had a new name.

Poppy

I wasn't exactly sure what these women were squealing about but they tossed me a few more of those buttery pillowy things so I just went along with it.

One's first night in a new home, or any home for that matter, can be weird. I thought I would be so happy, and I was but at the same time, things felt strange. I thought I should be out there, scrounging for food like I always do. I burped and the sweet taste of cinnamon invaded my taste buds. I sighed. I could get used to this, but at the same time, I knew it would take time.

I had finally fallen asleep, dreaming of those meatballs again when I heard a whirring sound. I opened one eye, groaned and closed it. It didn't stop, it sounded like the time a bee was after me, so I forced both eyes open and there was the human who dropped the popcorn, on this device that I could only describe as a torture chamber. She was poised on it, with her rump on a small pointy seat, and her legs were peddling two wheels in consistent circles. That poor thing! What beast was holding her against her will, forcing her to run for her life, never getting anywhere? I got up and moved closer to the two moving wheels. They scared me, but I needed to save her from her captor. I whined and whined until she finally hopped off. Phew. Good thing I was there or she'd be going in circles forever. And that is no way to live!

Pamela

"I'm sorry girl, did I wake you?" She patted the dog's big broad head. The dog looked up at her with what felt like pity, which was odd, since she was the one who had been a stray her whole life. She wondered what went through their heads….

"I think my Peloton freaked your dog out."

"Ugh, are you still doing that thing? You keep plenty in shape with yoga!"

"It's good cardio. Sorry if I scared your dog."

"She ain't my dog. I'm just keeping her until…."

"Don't lie to yourself, Peach."

"What did you just call me?"

"You heard me."

"Nobody has called me that in years."

"You lost your name when you lost yourself."

"I didn't lose myself, I just…"

"Right, you didn't lose yourself, just like that, over there isn't your dog."

"You're not making this easy."

"Iron sharpens iron baby. Now get dressed, we're going to be late for yoga class!"

Peach

During class Patricia wished she were in a spin class instead. She loved co-teaching beginner's yoga with Pamela, but this workout wasn't intense enough for her this morning. Not the way she was feeling. Something inside her simmered until it felt like it would boil over.

After class she grabbed her keys, and headed towards Pamela's to pick up the dog.

"Where are you going in such a hurry?"

"The dog and I are going to do a thing."

"You're not going to drop her off at the shelter are you?"

"No. We're going to get revenge. It's about time Peach took her rightful place on the throne of my life!"

24

Peach drove to Pamela's, grabbed Poppy and took off for her house, or what was still her house until Sebastian got ahold of a lawyer. "Buddy boy, it's time to rain on your parade." She knew Sebastian was planning a "friendsgiving" of sorts for all of his office staff on Saturday night, and that he had asked Lillian, their housekeeper to buy $500 worth of food for the occasion. She was always starving after yoga. She was going to go to the supermarket to pick up a few items including some dog food and something for lunch but she had a better idea.

Parking at their address she unlocked the door, knowing he was at work. She opened the pantry and began grabbing items—the ones she knew were reserved for Saturday night. Salty olives, her favorite! Goat cheese, figs, crackers, peach jelly, jalapeno and cream cheese, charcuterie, goose liver pate? Ew. She gave that to the dog. Then she burst out laughing. That nasty pate he loved so much was almost fifty dollars a can! The dog had eaten it in thirty seconds.

Poppy

I don't know what got into this human but she was flaming mad. I swore I heard a growl, but that very well could have been my stomach. She threw this can on the ground and I assumed it was for me, so I got my snout into it, and while it probably wasn't as decadent as a meatball, I didn't complain either. This stuff was choice! Even as a stray I knew that. She tossed me a few bits of rotisserie chicken, my own personal love language, thank you, and a few pita chips. How ethnic! After we were done foraging I burped and gave my best doggy smile. We exited the shelter and I pulled the leash.

"Hang on a minute." I relieved myself, feeling much better. That was more than I had eaten in weeks.

Peach

Peach looked at the gift Poppy had left on his perfectly manicured lawn. "Happy Thanksgiving, Asshole! Here's hoping you step in it."

Poppy

I'm not sure what changed in her the day she fed me the chicken and I used the potty in front of the house but it did. We never went back to that house but as the days passed she didn't send me back to that awful building she took me the first day we met.

Chapter Two

Melody

Melody got into her car after work, the sharp wind biting her cheeks. She wished she had brought a warmer jacket, as the raincoat she had put on this morning was doing nothing for her now as the temperature had dropped from warm and rainy to cold and windy. Her phone dinged as she sat down in the plush driver's seat. *"Happy anniversary, love. Pizza tonight, fancy shmancy seafood dinner Saturday night when it warms up a bit?"* She smiled. He always read her mind. She texted back *"definitely"* with a pizza and shrimp emoji followed by a few red hearts.

She had married Flynn eight years ago. He was five years older than she was. She fell for his charming Irish accent and sparkling blue-green eyes. Flynn was kind and practical, two things she'd wished she was more of. He brought out the best in her, parts she had forgotten existed, as life tends to cover over the most brilliant parts of us.

She left the library parking lot as Alanis Morissette came on the radio. Melody smiled. She knew the younger people whom she worked with preferred the music of today but Melody was a nineties girl at heart and had grown to become unashamed of this part of who she was. She turned the radio up as a guy in a yellow Mustang swerved in front of her. She slammed the breaks, missing him by inches. She sighed and honked at the rudeness of some people. Why was everyone always in such a hurry?

She closed her eyes for a moment, opened them, and as she continued the rest of the drive home, her thoughts drifted to her father. He had passed away last year, and some days she missed him more than others. She remembered eight years ago when he walked her down the aisle. His short sweaty arm held on featherlight to her own. He was a man who failed to show physical affection yet he had a way of making you feel like you mattered the most. He toasted her and Flynn at the reception, his voice shaking. She remembered him taking a sip of champagne and saying "that's better" laughing nervously, as the wedding party laughed politely and smiled. Nobody cared that Stuart was not a natural public speaker because the words he chose to describe his daughter were ones nobody, especially Melody, would forget.

What did her father see in her that others seemed to miss? She knew Flynn thought highly of her but the rest of the world seemed to view her as being more in the way than anything else. She knew her mother loved her but it always seemed that no matter what Melody did, her mother wished she'd done more. She always seemed quietly disappointed though she would never admit it.

Her thoughts shifted from her father to her mother. She knew her mother had taken her father's death really hard. She wished she'd had more connections besides her father. It was hard on Melody being an only child because all of the responsibility of her father's funeral had fallen on her. Of course she didn't let her mother help and after they buried him it was up to her to settle his affairs, though he had lived a very simple life. He had a few thousand dollars in CDs and since she was the only child left behind they were hers and Flynn's. She kept them in a safe in the bank, for emergencies as she couldn't fathom spending them. It was all she had left of her father save a few keepsakes that she didn't donate to charity.

She opened the door to their brick ranch style house. Flynn had turned on some bouncy Irish fiddle music, partly as a joke because he knew that while she loved him, the music of his nation was not her favorite. But she smiled because even when he wanted to bug her, it meant he was thinking about her.

He came into the hall and gave her a kiss on the head. She pulled back and feigned a look of disgust. He laughed. "I know this music is too upbeat for your liking, as you prefer more angsty *Melodys*."

"Yes, that's me. Emo. Did you order pizza?"

He laughed. "You haven't even taken your coat off yet, which I may add is a bit light for tonight's forecast."

"Thank you but I already have a Jewish mother."

"Not with a sexy Irish accent." She pulled a face.

"That would be weird."

"Sausage and peppers?"

"Excuse me?"

"The pizza. Sausage and peppers?"

"I haven't even taken my coat off yet!" He gave her a dirty look and she laughed.

"You're impossible"

"Thank ya."

She looked over as Flynn had, as usual, fallen asleep to the Netflix movie they had chosen. She had suggested *Sleepless in Seattle* and he had obliged probably because he knew she'd prefer it and he didn't care, he knew he'd fall asleep anyway. She swore some days he had narcolepsy.

The next day Melody was at her desk at the library looking on the library website for a book Mr. Harris swore he had returned. *If you give a Mouse a Cookie*. The Harris's were frequent flyers at the County Library, and while they were a sweet family they had seven children who were constantly losing books. She shrugged. At least it meant they were reading, but it would be nice to not have to keep re ordering books that these people lost. Her phone buzzed and she turned it over, engrossed in her quest to find the Laura Numeroff classic.

"Here it is." Alexis, her coworker said as she placed the paperback on the table next to her. She looked up. "Nope it's a different copy, but close enough. Trust me I know little Hannah colored red crayon on Mouse's ears on the original, but thanks! At least we have one in stock.

Melody's phone buzzed again as she turned it over. That was odd. It was her mother's neighbor, Jenny Aarons. She wondered why she'd be calling in the middle of the afternoon. She also had a lot of work to do so let it go to voicemail.

When she got in her car at 5:00 she listened to the message. "Hi Melody, this is Jenny Aarons, you're mother's neighbor. I don't want to go into a lot of details in a voice message but there have been some concerns about your mother lately, please call me back when you get a chance. Thanks."

That's peculiar, she thought. She knew her mother watched Jenny's six-year-old daughter after school Monday thru Thursday, but what sort of concerns would they have? She always seemed to enjoy watching the little girl, and mom had been fine recently, right? In fact Melody couldn't remember the last time she had spoken to her mother, so she really had no idea how she was. She felt sad for a minute, as how could she have been so jaded as to allow life to get in the way to the point where she had failed to check on her mother? She knew she had been having a hard time with her father's death but then again who wouldn't? She loved her husband dearly, and Melody knew she hadn't been the most diligent in spending time with her since his passing. When she got home she called Jenny back.

"Hello?"

"Hi, Jenny, it's Melody, I got your voice message."

"Yes, hi, thanks for calling back."

"Is everything ok?"

"Well, not exactly. You know your mom watches Ebony after school on weekdays. They have a routine and every Tuesday Estelle makes her mac and cheese. This Tuesday Ebony told me that when she asked her about dinner she had no idea what she was talking about, and she almost seemed belligerent. Totally fine that she didn't make Ebony dinner, we could feed her at home, but it was the disappointment more than anything. Also, when I picked her up I noticed that your mother wasn't as immaculate as usual."

"How so?"

"It seemed to have been awhile since she had taken the garbage out. Her clothes looked like she had been wearing them the past few days. Again, no big deal, however I know your mom really likes to look nice so this was really out of character for her." Melody began to feel defensive. So, maybe mom hadn't been feeling well the past few days? Was that really a big deal? But in the back of her mind Melody knew that if it wasn't a concern the Aarons wouldn't have been calling her. They didn't know her super well, and they wouldn't just call a virtual stranger unless they were truly concerned.

"Melody? Are you there?"

"Yeah, sorry. I was just thinking. I'm really sorry she let you down in babysitting Ebony. I'll definitely talk to her. Thanks for letting me know."

"You're welcome. I hope everything is ok."

"So do I, thanks." She hung up her phone just as Flynn walked into the kitchen.

"Is everything ok?" He asked as he put a hand on her shoulder. She looked up.

"Oh, yeah, I think so. I just got this strange phone call from Jenny Aarons, my mother's next door neighbor. She mentioned that mom seemed different than usual. Less organized and unkempt. And she forgot the little girl's favorite dinner Tuesday night? I'm sure it's nothing, but I'll give her a call this weekend."

Friday evening could not come soon enough. Melody kept checking her phone for the time at work, hoping for 4:30 to arrive. She and Flynn had not had a nice dinner out in forever and tonight they would be celebrating their anniversary at their favorite restaurant, Ocean Prime. It was downtown, and had the best seafood. She looked over at Phoebe reading to the kids at story time. Phoebe's position was part time, as she was a college student studying to be an English teacher. Melody knew she could not afford to have a part time job, though she would kill to do something like that. While she and Flynn had never had children of their own, and while she wasn't sure she wanted them, she enjoyed being around them and would love a chance to use her creativity to arrange the story time. She knew Phoebe did a nice job, but also that when she graduated next year, she would leave and the library would hire another college student for the same job, and people would float through the library doing something she wanted to do, but did not have the luxury of pursuing. She sighed. Why did she have such a habit of lamenting and settling? Maybe that was the thing that her mother saw in her that she wished would change. Maybe her mother was right.

She had spritzed perfume on her neck as he came into the bedroom.

"Help. I'm bad at this," he said, holding up his tie.

31

"You don't have to wear a tie for me!"

"I know, I wanted to, the clothes horse in me is tired of every day at work being 'casual Friday.' Maybe I'm an old fashioned European but I like to dress nice for my woman once in a while!"

"I'm your woman, huh? Ok, I'll help you look dapper."

"You look lovely as well. "

"Thanks. I could go to work in sweats too if I wanted to. It's silly the way people dress today like they rolled out of bed. Oh God, I sound old."

He laughed. "That's ok, your date is even older."

"Cradle robber."

"I found the cutest one in the cradle."

She loved the awkward way he flirted with her, his Irish lilt accenting the charm. She'd won big with Flynn, and she knew it. He was one of the few things in her life that she felt she had done right. It seemed like the men in her life, her husband, and her late father had been in her corner, and always would be. Yet the women, her mother, friends she had fallen out of touch with for one reason or another, and even her boss, never did much for her self-esteem. But tonight, she thought, as she fastened a pearl earring, she would celebrate what was good in her life.

"Damn these earrings are pulling. I usually only wear studs."

"You're sitting next to a stud." he smiled. "I hear you though. This tie is a bit binding."

"I'm sorry. Did I make it too tight? I really didn't mean to strangle you!"

"Not your fault. I'm not used to dressing up, but what's a bit of discomfort over being the best dressed couple here?"

She turned around to see a couple in their twenties, the girl's light blue satin dress perfectly accenting her figure, and the guy's tie perfectly matching her dress. They smiled excitedly, as it was probably their first time at this very choice establishment. *Ok.* She thought to herself, *the best dressed couple over forty!*

After a wonderful dinner and two glasses of wine, one more than she usually imbibed, Melody and Flynn didn't get to bed until midnight, so when her phone rang at 9:00 am she was just waking up. The number was unknown, but something inside her told her to answer it anyway.

"Hello?" She knew her voice sounded garbled, as if it was thick from sleep.

"Mrs. Malley?"

"This is her."

"Hi, my name is Jesse Barnes. I'm the assistant manager at Safeway on South Broadway. It seems your mother is here and she's very disoriented. She said she forgot how she got here, and when we ask her where she lives, she just keeps repeating that she's forgotten how she got here. She hadn't made any purchases. It seems she's also forgotten why she came here in the first place. Can somebody come and pick her up and take her home?"

After apologizing, though for what, she wasn't sure, and promising to come as soon as possible, she hung up the phone, stunned. This was the second phone call she had received this week in regards to her mother's mental state. She didn't know what to think as she got dressed. Flynn had just gotten out of the shower.

"Morning, love. Wow, I feel better! I was sure I stank of lobster from last night, but was too lazy to shower when we got in." He looked at her worried expression. "Is something the matter?"

"I just got another phone call about Mom. This time from Safeway. The manager said she was at the grocery store this morning confused and disoriented. Said she didn't know where she was and he asked could somebody please come and get her."

"Oh my."

"Yes, I don't know what's going on with her. This is the woman who tells me to 'tuck my shirt in. I look like a slob,' and now her neighbor's calling me and telling me that she hasn't changed clothes in days and that she hasn't taken the garbage out. It just doesn't make sense."

"Well, let's go up there and see what all the fuss is about. I'm guilty as a bad son-in-law, I've not spoken to her in a while myself."

"I know, but I'm her daughter, it's definitely my responsibility to be there for her, especially since dad passed away. I know she's been lonely, but I let my busy life and my own self-obsession get in the way of it."

They arrived at the Safeway and one of the baggers was sitting with her mother on the bench across from the customer service desk. The girl, who was no more than eighteen, was doing a fine job of trying to talk to Estelle, but to no avail.

"Mrs. Clayton, I think this is your daughter coming up. Are you ready to go home now?" Her mother didn't answer, nor did she look up when Melody and Flynn stood in front of her.

"Mom, is everything ok?" Dumb question, Melody thought to herself. Of course she wasn't ok. Her mother was usually independent and would never ger flustered by something as simple as a grocery store trip.

"Hi, Mrs. Malley, thank you for coming." Jesse Barnes greeted them. "Mrs. Clayton, your daughter and son-in-law will be taking you home now."

Melody cringed at the volume in which Mr. Barnes spoke to her mother. Her mother was seventy- five years old. Up until this point she had kept a perfect home, raised a daughter, taught mahjong, volunteered at an animal rescue center and helped new dog owners train their dogs. She wasn't a moron or deaf and this twenty-five-year-old boy didn't need to be yelling in her ear. She cringed inwardly. But at the same time, all he saw in her was a very confused old woman who wasn't fit to shop alone. At that moment, she wished the world, herself included, knew her mom for who she really was.

Flynn offered to sit in the back so Estelle could ride shotgun, but she refused. All she kept asking about was when were they going to get her car? Had she done something wrong? Would she be able to drive again?"

"We'll see, mom" was the only answer she could offer her for now. She had no idea how her mother had gotten to this state, and as she looked at her from the front seat she saw a shadow of the woman she once knew. Her hair was out of place, and only a month ago she would have perished the thought of skipping a trip to the salon. Now she looked like she hadn't combed her hair in a week, and her outfit seemed like she had been wearing it for a few days.

When they got to her house, the smell greeting them from the hallway was pungent, to put it mildly. Flynn covered his mouth and coughed. "Good Lord, it smells....." he stopped himself, put his hand on Estelle's shoulder then went to take out the garbage without another word. Melody wanted to judge her mother, scold her for not caring for herself properly, but following her husband's much more compassionate example, she instructed her mother to have a seat, as she went to work cleaning the kitchen. The kitchen didn't take long as there was no food in it, just a few counters to wipe down and something that looked like sand on the floor. Looking in the refrigerator, Melody realized that there was very little food in it, save for a pat of butter, a quarter full bottle of prune juice, and a shriveled lime.

Groceries! In their haste to leave the embarrassing situation, they had forgotten to get what their mother had come for. Groceries.

"Hey, Melody, why don't we drive to the store, pick up mom's car? You can drive it back here, and I'll stay behind to pick up a bit of food."

"Great plan." she responded, grateful that someone other than her was arranging the details. Estelle followed wordlessly along with whatever she or Flynn suggested, but when they arrived at the parking lot she insisted on driving.

"Mom, do you really think that's a good idea? I mean you..."

"Don't tell me what's a good idea and what's not, Melody! Who raised who? Just because I had a rough morning doesn't mean I'm not perfectly capable of driving myself home. Why don't you stay with him?" she pointed, referring to Flynn. "And I'll drive home."

"Mam, why don't you come with me and pick out some groceries, and Melody will drive your car to the house?"

"Why doesn't Melody drive her car to the house and I'll drive us home after the shopping?" Flynn looked at her and nodded. It was a good compromise, considering Flynn was much more collected in situations like this.

As she drove her car back to her mom's she reflected on the past nine months since her father's passing. While he had never officially converted to Judaism upon marrying Estelle, Stuart had immersed himself in the Jewish faith and culture, and to honor his life the funeral was a Jewish one, as she knew that was what he wanted. She knew that after the funeral, Melody and Flynn had moved on. They went back to their everyday lives, leaving Estelle alone with very little support from the community. The rabbi offered his number if Estelle ever felt like she needed someone to talk to, but being the proud woman that she was, Melody knew her mother would never take him up on the offer. The truth was that it wasn't the job of the bereaved to reach out to others, but for the community to pursue them as they so needed. Besides her very concerned neighbors, her mother had none of that. She felt angry with herself. She was so upset with her negligence. No wonder her mother pished on her floor and left her or Flynn mop it up. And here she was obviously very mentally unwell and she was just now learning of it. She also reasoned that her mother could have called *her* letting her know she wasn't feeling right, but she knew that ultimately, she was the one who needed to check on her mother before the neighbor and finally the grocery store manager contacted her.

She arrived back at the house and began making room for groceries in the cupboard, which was unnecessary, since they were virtually bare. She wandered into her mother's room. The bed was unmade, which was unusual but there was something else odd about the room. Every single picture and keepsake from her mother and father's life, beginning with their wedding was either on her dresser or strewn on the floor.

Melody began picking up the pictures. Pictures of her with her cousins at various holiday gatherings, as well as a picture of her and her father when she caught her first fish in the Colorado River. Her father was no sportsman, but did have an affinity for fishing and he had passed that on to her in her youth.

She sighed as she knew that she should be deeply worried about her mother at this moment, and she was, however she couldn't help miss her father even more. This had always been the case, even when she was a child.

"Mommy, when is daddy coming home? I got a new book at school. I want to read it with him. Her mother smiled. "He's at work, why don't you go into your room, do your homework and you two can read it after dinner. Excuse me." she said as she picked up the phone to make a call.

Melody sighed. She knew there was no point in asking Mom to read with her. She was always too 'busy.'

36

At that moment Melody had many mixed emotions. She knew she had not been devoted to her mother, way before she got ill, even when her father was ill. When her father had begun to show signs of his illness, she'd shied away. She couldn't bear to see her father in that state, and she was terrified of her mother seeing her vulnerability. So she kept "busy". She did the same thing her mother had done to her when she was a child. Whenever Melody had gone to her mom for anything as a child her mom had made an excuse not to help her. Now, whenever her mom reached out for anything, Melody made the same excuse about having too much to do, even going so low as to lie and say Flynn needed her support right now, while she knew her husband wanted more than anything for her to be with her family.

"We're home!" Flynn called from the living room. Melody ran into the room knowing she had done a pretty lax job in tidying up her mother's home, as she had made even more of a mess in her bedroom, looking through the photos. At least, she had cleaned the kitchen.

Flynn, as usual, had taken over and purchased some good healthy groceries for Estelle. He smiled as he unpacked the bags and Melody had two simultaneous thoughts. One that her husband was amazing, and that how on earth could they be spending their Saturday afternoon in a home helping a woman who just two short years ago organized fundraisers for animal rescue? Now she couldn't remember why she had come to the grocery store, and needed help picking out food. This was the woman who'd insisted Melody eat healthy every day when she was a child. She shook her head. Of course some people decline as they age, but somehow, she never imagined this happening to her own mother, not the woman who was always more put together and on top of things than Melody ever was.

On Tuesday, after much coercing from Flynn, Melody took the afternoon off work to take her mother to a neurologist. On the way there Melody did her best to encourage her mother to answer the doctor's questions in a way that would prove to her that she was perfectly fine, and just having a bad day on Sunday, was all. Looking over at her mother, who was even more despondent then she had been on Sunday, she knew that there was no way that that was going to happen.

Dr. Anders, the neurologist, asked her mother a series of questions, and Estelle was either unable or unwilling to answer most of them. She sat next to her mother, across from the very grim physician, as he shook his head and explained:

"I've done some brain scans on Mrs. Clayton and unfortunately I've found quite a bit of beta amyloid. That paired with your mother's age as well as her cognitive aptitude shown in the test we took today means that I have unfortunately diagnosed her with Alzheimer's.

Melody was in shock. She attempted to explain to her mother what this meant, and as she did her mother nodded weakly, but as to whether or not she understood, well that was inconclusive. In fact, her mother said very little in the two hours she was in the office taking the tests. This made Melody wonder how the hell the doctor could come up with any conclusion at all. Could he be wrong? But Dr. Anders did not seem like the kind of person that one would argue with, especially not a person as passive as Melody felt she was. She wished her mother was here, and upon that thought realized that she was. She was there, right beside her, physically, but she was not the woman she remembered.

Melody lay on the couch that evening, her head on Flynn's lap. She had reluctantly dropped her mother off at home. She asked her if she would be ok, and her mother had nodded, which was of little comfort, as she had been nodding all afternoon, with little else to indicate that she had understood anything that had taken place.

"I just don't understand it. How on earth could I have missed so much of her cognitive decline? Had she been like this after my father's death? Before? My God I'm such a horrible daughter."

Her father's funeral had been a blur, and the only time she had remembered interacting with her mother at all was when they had stood side by side as the rabbi offered his prayers in the burial service and they both threw a shovel full of dirt into his open grave. She shuddered at the memory.

Stuart Clayton had not been raised in a Jewish home, but he had unofficially converted when he had married Estelle. As neither was particularly religious, their family life consisted of a series of random Jewish celebrations whenever they felt up to it. While not an official religious holiday, Stuart had always admired the celebration of Tu BiShvat, as he was an avid nature lover, and cared deeply about the environment. She had memories of his hands over hers as they dug a hole in the dirt to place a new sapling, as snow softly fell around them.

Since her father had been diagnosed with prostate cancer in 2017, Melody had been running. Running from her father's prognosis, running from the responsibility as the only child to help her mother with her father's care. She had arranged a trip to Ireland to visit Flynn's parents a few months before her father was diagnosed, and once she learned of his diagnosis, she had failed to tell Flynn right away, as she knew that the news would cause him to cancel their trip. Once they had gone on the trip, and arrived back home, she told him the news, and he was furious.

"Dammit Melody! They're my family too, and in your parents' time of need we, myself unknowingly, ran off, and left them to process this on their own. I think it was selfish."

She remembered her stomach dropping at his response. Of all the people in the world, Flynn was the one she wanted to disappoint the least.

In the last few years of her father's life Melody visited infrequently—at home, when he was hospitalized and finally when he was sent home for palliative care. Each of those times she had avoided eye contact or conversation with her father the best she could. She spoke to her mother over the logistics of her father's care and current prognosis. She helped straighten up the house. At the hospital she got into long discussions with the nurses about absolutely nothing at all. She took Flynn with her whenever possible, and whenever he attempted to engage Stuart in conversation, she would interrupt and start a separate conversation with Flynn. She was being a brat and she knew it, and looking back she felt terribly regretful. Now, with her mother facing even more loss, she had no idea how she was going to face this new reality.

Chapter Three

Peach

After her trip back home to sabotage Sebastian's upcoming dinner, Peach was feeling empowered. She looked at the dog at her feet, as she and Pamela shared a bottle of white wine. It was a pleasant evening for November in Denver and they were sitting outside of one of their favorite cafes on the heated back porch.

"Any more thoughts about what you're going to do with the dog? " Pamela asked.

This made Peach smirk. Her friend knew exactly what she was going to do. After this afternoon's escapade she and Poppy were officially partners in crime. They had broken bread together as well as deboned a chicken. They were forever united.

The more time she spent with Poppy the more potential she saw in her to do great things. What those great things were she wasn't quite sure.

She and Pamela shared a bottle of wine as a sort of celebration of Peach's recent exodus as well as Pam's 1000th bag of popcorn produced and sold. Their first inclination had been to go to a fancy indoor restaurant, however since Poppy had everything to do with the current order of celebration they couldn't very well leave her out. So they opted for an outdoor cafe where dogs were more than welcome under their heated tent.

"You should train her."

"I never could train my husband."

Pamela winked. "He wasn't as treat motivated. She really listens to you."

"Bacon snacks help. She definitely isn't Jewish!" Pamela laughed.

"Maybe just not observant. But you've got a sweet little filly here. I've never had a dog so I really have nothing to compare her to. But…. remember when we went to New Mexico? When we visited the Navajo tribe, they were talking about how the wolf symbolized medicine. As if they have healing powers. I know it's been a long time since we've been there. I don't know about you, but I truly believe that each animal has some sort of role in human existence. Hell, even the beetle has some sort of symbolism."

"That's because you believe in all that hocus pocus."

"You used to believe in that hocus pocus too until your husband ridiculed you to the point where you stopped believing in anything. Honestly it's up to us what God we follow if any. I don't have a problem with being an atheist but if you look to a person as your ultimate God you're in trouble."

"I never did intend to make him my God, I didn't even like him, but Pamela do you know why I think I stayed with this jokester so long?"

"Enlighten me."

"My parents hated Sebastian. In the beginning I totally opposed them because he was so exciting and wonderful. I mean he was a jerk but he was an exciting jerk. Then he really began to show his true colors. That or he had always shown his true colors and I was too blind to see them until one day I was not. I don't even know the day or moment I realized that he was my greatest mistake but sadly it was quite a while ago. It took his bossy 'get me some razors' and a random stray dog to help me realize that I needed to do something I should have done twenty five years ago."

"Well," said Pamela, "I've not been a licensed professional counselor for the past five years, however you're wining and dining me so I suppose I can indulge your musings. I knew Sebastian was no good since day one, but I'm not the sort of person who is going to tell someone what they should or shouldn't do. So I sat by and supported you no matter what. While you supported me. You've always supported me. You always supported Sebastian. Now it's your turn. What do you want to do, Peach? Looking at this dog, what do you see for her? I know she didn't just come into your life to be your fellow couch potato though I have nothing against Netflix and chill. I truly believe she has some sort of purpose, but then again I've always believed in that hocus pocus!"

Peach raised a glass. "Here's to whatever the universe has in store for me and Poppy. And to Pam's 1000th pop!"

"I've got it!" Pam exclaimed as she ran into the living room after teaching yoga.

"You're sweaty."

"I'm excited. So Tina knows this gal, I forgot her name and she trains dogs. She trains them for various occupations, like this woman is a miracle worker. But what she really specializes in is therapy dogs."

"Therapy dogs?"

"Therapy dogs." Pamela laughed. "We could go back and forth with this all day but yes, she trains dogs to visit different facilities, you know, to come and cheer up hospital patients and all that. I think Poppy has a chance. What they do is evaluate the dog, do all the hand in the face tests, etc. I don't know much about this, but basically make sure the dog is kosher, not aggressive, and has a good temperament. The biggest thing they test for is response to external stimuli. They open the umbrella near its face, the fake hand next to their food bowl, and get this, a doll that's the size of a young child and they make it act like a child. Kind of forward, in the dog's space and all that. If your dog passes they go to phase two."
"Phase two. Sounds so official"

"Oh, it is." Pamela looked at Poppy. "Can you do it, girl? Can you endure umbrellas, fake hands, crazy, fake kids all in this big open room. Just don't freak out or you might blow it."

"Well, no pressure. Pamela, do you really think Poppy is cut out for this? Up until last week she lived on the mean streets of Denver, not knowing where her next meal was coming from. Can she really go from a scared stray to a miracle medicine dog?"

"I don't know. Can you go from a submissive married woman to divorced bad-ass dog trainer and hospital miracle worker?"

"Who are you calling submissive?"

"Who are you calling a scared little stray?"

"Touché."

Poppy

There's a point in every dog's life when she goes from huddling under some tree to escape the next thunderstorm to wearing her first collar. It must have been some collar because the two females I found myself in the company of made this oohing sound, like a bunch of happy wolves. I suppose if I managed to get this sort of contraption on another species I'd feel triumphant as well but in their defense I'd do anything for a puffed caramel corn.

"We need to stop feeding her this crap. It's going to make her sick. She needs real dog treats. I know she loves beef jerky, that's how I got her into my car the first day. Not that Pam's Pops are crap. They're delicious, but maybe not so good for a dog."

"Atsa Jewish mother! Don't worry most dogs respond just as well to their kibble as a treat than a treat itself. We can use that until we get some actual treats."

"We went into the moving box again. There was no need to coax me with a treat to get me into one of those again, because ever since we went to the chicken and liver house and ate all that good food, I trust the moving box completely. But now we were in the box and we stopped at this building. I looked up. It was big and I saw another dog going into it. Oh no, it's not that awful place I went to with her the first night, is it? But the dog seemed to want to go into the building. All of the humans and dogs walking in and out of this building seemed happy to be there and I didn't have the same sense of foreboding. Plus the human ladies seemed very excited; I didn't smell a molecule of fear. Except maybe a little bit from me.

The place was big and it smelled like beef. The humans were standing at some counter barking to one another over something, and I spotted this Great Dane right next to me.

"Hey."

He turned. "What's up?"

"This place. What's it like? Is it good?"

"It's cool, bro. You get all these treats for listening just like at home. They put all this stuff in your face and if you're all chill about it they give you more snacks. If you freak out they coo at you, 'oh, it's ok' like you're a puppy again. Then when you get all done they train you."

"What's training?"

He looked at me with his head to the side. "What, were you raised in a cave? Training means they make you do stuff for snackies. Then when you're done you get to go cheer up old people or sick kids or something. It's great."

"I cheer people up? How do I do that?'

"Go look in the mirror toots. You're a dog. People love us. It's like we're cute or something. They call me Teddy. Because I'm their big old teddy bear. They can call me what they want if they keep giving me beef bits."

"My name's Poppy. Thanks for the 411, Teddy."

"No problem. Good luck."

"Thanks."

Teddy wasn't entirely wrong, though he wasn't very thorough. Maybe he didn't know the word for umbrella. Poor chap. I hope he passed his umbrella test. I passed mine. I think it was because that big jar of beef was right there, and I was thinking more about it than the scary umbrella. Then they gave me some kibble! It was like a restaurant. So here I was munch munch munch, and something that looked like a hand but didn't smell like one tried to take the bowl away. Kind of annoying, but if it was trying to be a real hand why did it smell like plastic? I did nothing and was rewarded with "good girl!" and given more beefy bites. This was great so far.

Then came the ultimate test. The human took this plush looking doll and walked it towards me like it was real. It started making these high pitched sounds and barking in human language only like how a human puppy would.

"Hi doggy. Can I pet you? Aw, cute doggy!"

I shrugged and licked the fabric arm. If this was supposed to annoy me these people had never heard a blue jay. Imagine having hearing that's four times better than a human and having to hear those things carry on all day! This human pretending to sound squeaky was nothing compared to that. I even sat to get a rise out of them. As expected they all squealed and gave me some more beef. This was easy.

After that, all the humans shook paws. I'm not fluent in English but I heard the phrase "good dog" a few times and some laughter over how much I liked treats. I rolled my eyes. Have any of them ever been homeless? You'd be going after those beef bites too!

Peach

As they drove home Peach thought about how far Poppy had come in the short time. She was so proud of her for passing the preliminary test. After that they would be "interviewed" by potential trainers and discuss what sort of service to enroll her in. If a scared little stray could come so far she knew she could grow too. At that moment she wished she had the resilience of a dog. They don't hold grudges. They don't have doubts or regrets. All they want out of life are snacks and affection. She thought of the ninety-plus dogs that were housed at the shelter she'd taken Poppy to be scanned. For some reason she couldn't help thinking about the fate of each one. She hoped each one would get their own backyard to romp around in and play fetch. The realist in her knew that not every dog would have that outcome. But in that moment, she decided to rejoice that Poppy did.

Chapter Four

Melody

"Well this is nice." Flynn drawled as they entered the lobby of the Sunshine Estate, the nursing facility that Dr. Anders had suggested to them once it was evident that Estelle was no longer safe at home, on her own.

Melody walked slowly as her mother held onto her elbow, though she was perfectly capable of walking on her own. Over the past few weeks, though there was nothing physically wrong with her back or legs, Estelle's mobility had decreased significantly. Dr. Anders explained that that sometimes happens with Alzheimer's patients. Looking around Melody had to admit that this place wasn't as gross as she had expected. It smelled like Salisbury steak but the interior design was pleasant. No archaic looking artwork on the walls, as other places she had visited had. She remembered visiting her grandfather when she was fifteen. He was in hospice care in a nursing home. He was still as sharp as a tack until his final hours on Earth, however the woman in the room next to him kept yelling "help me!!" every five minutes as her family was trying to say their final goodbyes to their beloved dad and grandpa. Looking around the lobby, while there were people in wheelchairs, and some looking pretty confused there were no frantic screams. At least not so far.

She pulled the nurse acting as tour guide aside, employing Flynn to temporarily hold onto her mother.

"Excuse me?"

The nurse, Hannah smiled. "Yes?"

"I know many nursing facilities have a memory care unit. I don't know if you are aware but my mother has been diagnosed with Alzheimer's and it is no longer safe for her to live at home, hence why she is here. Is this section of the building for dementia patients?"

Hannah smiled. "Here at the Sunshine Estate we don't group patients into particular units. We feel that will limit their care. Every single one of our staff from CNAs to nurses to even our doctors in residence are trained in memory care. If they are caring for a patient with dementia or Alzheimer's they are trained to meet those particular needs, however, we don't like to label patients and put them in a box. So we have individuals with dementia on the same wing as those here for more physically related reasons. There are even a few individuals here in physical therapy who are staying for a specific amount of time until they are rehabilitated. Some of them are rather young. I hope that answers your question."

"Yes, very thoroughly, thank you."

"I need Melody." Estelle stated plainly as she'd had enough of Flynn supporting her overall physically steady frame.

"I'm here, Mom." she said as she released Flynn from his duties.

He wandered over to the bulletin. "Look over here, love. They say they have therapy dogs visiting here every Wednesday, Thursday and Friday. It's through a program called "Pals for Patients". It sounds lovely but I'll make a point not to come those days. Though I know mam loves animals, she may enjoy it."

"Do you not like animals?" Hannah asked Flynn.

"I love them, I'm just deathly allergic to dogs and to a lesser extent cats." Just then he sneezed. He grabbed a tissue from the front desk to blow his nose. "Wow, I feel some allergies coming on now, almost like I've been exposed to cat hair."

"We do have a cat in residence. His name is Mac. The residents love him." She handed him a mask. "This might help. I'm a bit allergic too so I wear one from time to time."

Flynn donned the mask. Just then a gray tabby slinked up to them. Flynn laughed. "Right on time."

Estelle looked at Flynn and turned to Melody. "Why is he wearing a blanket over his face all of a sudden?"

"Mom, there's a cat who lives here and Flynn is allergic, remember? Look, there it is." The big cat slinked by and Melody reached down to pet him. "Mom, you love cats. Do you want to pet him?"

"I can't bend, you know that!"

Hannah smiled. "Mac makes his rounds. He may come and visit you, Mrs. Clayton. He can tell who the animal lovers are."

"I never had a cat."

"Mom, you've always had cats."

Flynn looked at her and shook his head behind his mask. His face was covered but she could read his eyes. Now wasn't the time. She sighed. She looked at her mother and the cold reality hit her that she was dealing with a completely different person than the one she once knew.

Chapter Five

Poppy

Teddy was right. We went through some pretty intensive training. Those humans looked exhausted. I on the other hand kept getting treats thrown my way for doing the littlest thing. Boy was I getting fat. It was nice to have someone proud of me.

One night I heard a rumbling. There had been some white stuff coming down all week but it had gotten warmer. The sky got this color I didn't like then the sun went down. The humans had gone to sleep and I was on my pillow dozing off when I heard this rumbling. It sounded like a bear but I knew it was coming from the sky. Then the sky lit up. Darn I'd seen this before. Once the bright stuff got so close it split open the abandoned shed I was staying in to keep dry. Then the shed lit up and there was all this hot orange stuff around it. I ran for my life then. I hoped that didn't happen tonight. I really didn't want the popcorn ladies' shelter to ignite with us in it.

Peach

She dreamt she was in Boulder with Sebastian. They were at this concert and he was holding her hand. The music was perfect and the evening was temperate. Then all of the sudden a literal boulder came rolling towards them. More specifically it was rolling towards her. She looked closer and the boulder had Sebastian's features chiseled into it. It kept rolling faster and she attempted to run. But he wouldn't let go of her hand. "You're mine." he said over and over again no matter how hard she pulled.

Finally she broke free and ran as fast as she could until she woke up. She turned over panting loudly. She looked at the clock. 3:03. Outside, the thunder rumbled. She heard Poppy whimpering outside her bedroom door. She nosed her way in and hopped on the bed. She put her hand on her rough head and drew her towards her.

Ever since her bath she smelled more like lavender and less like every trash can she had ever visited. She closed her eyes and she gently put her arms around her thick neck. They were both safe.

Chapter Six

Melody

"I hate leaving her there, Flynn." She said this woodenly though the emotions within her were a raging storm.

When you have a good sound relationship with a loved one, and when they go through a demise the tears often flow freely over the loss of what was. However, when one has a relationship that is strained, the undoing of one of the individuals in the relationship causes a flurry of emotions that are hard to define, hard to grasp. Melody felt like her mom was going through this and she was her only source of help and comfort, and she was not who her mother preferred. The only one who'd understood her mother, who'd loved her fully, was the same one who'd loved and understood Melody fully. Her father. His death had caused a displacement and despondency in Estelle that seemed to come on quickly, stealing the best parts of her.

"Melody, I know this sounds odd," Flynn stated, "But do you really think Mam has Alzheimer's? I'm not a physician, not a neurologist but her decline was so…rapid."

"I know, but Dr. Anders said that can happen at her age, and the grief of losing Dad could also have advanced her symptoms."

Melody didn't want to go back to the nursing home, didn't want to see her mother in that state, didn't want to face the disappointment that was their failed relationship, the guilt that somehow her emotional neglect of her mother brought on this disease that had been looming in her body, looking for a crack to emerge from and erase everything her mother once was. Melody lay on her bed and wept bitterly, mourning a woman, lost and confused, not her mother, but Melody herself. Never before had she felt so much like a helpless orphan, and so incredibly burdened by her mother's future."

The next Saturday she sat in her armchair, nursing her coffee, afraid to do what she knew needed to be done.

"Melody Lynne Clayton, I'm not going to Sunshine Estate donning an N95 and making small talk with your despondent mother on my own. I love you but you know you're being a selfish brat as well as I do. I will never stop loving you. But please don't make me drag you kicking and screaming. I'll do it."

She tried to hide a smile, as she held her coffee cup and looked deep into her phone absorbing herself in something she didn't care about on Facebook. She was dressed and had breakfast but she didn't want to take the next step. But she had no choice. Her stomach churned and jumped and her heart palpitated at the image of her mother in her mind, but she knew she had to force her feet to do their thing, because she was an adult. She was also a child, the only child of a woman who had been disappointed in her her entire life.

Poppy

We were in this new place. It smelled like steak that had been cooking for too long. And potatoes. Lots of potatoes. I looked around. Most of the humans smelled like they were over the age of eleven dog years. Seniors. What was this? A human puppy! He was cute and smiling so I licked him, which made him giggle. He tasted like maple syrup. His mother reached over to pet me too. Good vibe from her but she had this stupid smelling hand lotion. Yuck, the little hand tasted better. I like human puppies. They were always sticky and sweet.

I did my best to mind my human, though there was so much to see. Unlike a lot of places we've gone to, parks, doggy/human bars(those are the best) and just the busy streets of Denver this place was really quiet aside from a few giggles from the human puppy and the old people he was with. Some official looking people were walking around wheeling carts with little bottles on them but they were moving pretty slowly.

Then I heard it. "Hissssss." I looked up. Perched on a couch cushion was the brattiest looking little pisser I'd ever seen. I ignored him, putting my tail in their air, hoping he'd smell my confidence.

"Psst. Hey, mutt." Oh, I know that cat wasn't talking to me. "You think you're special roaming this place but guess what? This is my territory. Don't make me pee on the carpet because I will."

I rolled my eyes. That will make the people who work here happy. I thought sarcastically. Cats really were a trip.

"I'm not scared of any silly little mutt, especially because this is my living room. Everyone here pets me and tells me I'm a sweet boy. I don't need no skinny little pup stealing my attention."

I looked up. "Dude, I'm a dog. I go where the human takes me. She's my alpha. She doesn't even like cats." I had no idea if this was true but he didn't need to know differently.

I ignored the puss through the rest of the walk. When you have four legs and a chatty human who literally has to sniff every other human she meets, the destination takes a long time. Humans are a journey species, for them it's all about the trip. For dogs it's all about getting to where you want to go, especially if you have to go potty.

We finally entered this small room. It was a sad room. There were three humans in it. One was standing, and two were sitting. One of the seats had wheels on them. I like the boxes with wheels better than I used to but lone wheels still make me nervous. As a stray you have no idea how many boxes with wheels almost turned me into roadkill. Drivers don't look. But these wheels weren't moving. They seemed big compared to the chair they were attached to. The standing human was male and was wearing what looked like a muzzle. I wonder who he bit. The sitting female was quiet and she smelled a little scared. Nobody smelled mean. All good vibes but everyone seemed sad. I sniffed the female in the chair with wheels. I smelled…nothing. Sure there was this decadent looking meatloaf on a plate next to her that I wanted to get my mouth on but coming from the human herself, nothing. Oh no. I've seen this before. Once I approached a stray and I sensed nothing from him. Turns out he was dead! Was this poor human dead? I pulled the leash closer and saw her blink. No, not dead. But why was she so quiet? Why was everyone so quiet? I looked at my human and sniffed. I smelled a little fear but some determination too. I wasn't sure what I was supposed to do. The only thing I wanted to do in that room was eat the meatloaf!

Peach

It was day one at Sunshine Estates where she and Poppy were going to visit the residents and it had been a long time since Peach felt this nervous. There were times when Sebastian had made her nervous, but those feelings switched over to defeat so quickly she never had a chance to embrace the feeling for long. She looked down at Poppy. She had her head tilted to one side, a curious look on her face. She wished it were socially acceptable for humans to sniff a situation like it was for dogs because her eyes and ears weren't telling her much. She remembered what she learned in yoga. Pamela told her that you could turn any situation into a yoga studio if you so desired. Peach figured this statement probably didn't apply to war zones, but a busy yet quiet nursing facility could be a place of deep contemplation and relaxation if one so chose to make it such. She took a deep breath and briefly closed her eyes. She rolled her eyes behind her lids. *These people are going to think I'm nuts*, she thought, standing here channeling the muses or something. Damn, she wished she were a bolder person. She'd been as bold as extra hot picante at one point in her life, but years of living under the tyranny that was Sebastian had robbed so much from her. *Bullshit*, she thought. *He stole nothing from me. I just forgot who I was, is all, but it doesn't mean I've **changed**! I'm still me and I've got this.*

"Hello!" she chirped as she stepped further into the room. She had no idea what she was expecting. Maybe a wizened old woman sitting up in bed knitting, smiling, and summoning her to bring that adorable dog closer so she could meet her. Instead she was met with two forty somethings looking stoic and an old woman sitting in a wheelchair looking despondent.

"My name is Patricia but you can call me Peach. This is Poppy. I know—a lot of Ps! Poppy and I are here to say hi. I don't know if any of you are dog lovers, but Poppy might change your mind. She certainly changed mine. I was not looking for a dog, but we found each other.

Melody

This lady with the dog made Melody sad. When Mom was in her right mind she would light up whenever she saw anything with four legs. Dogs were her passion. The big fat puss who lived at this facility had slinked in here a few times and Mom totally ignored him, but the fact that she didn't respond to a dog in her room, to Melody felt almost as if she was dead.

"Mom, look at the dog. Isn't she cute? You love dogs."

Nothing. She shook her head and looked at the lady. "I'm sorry. My mother has Alzheimer's, she's not herself."

"I understand." Patricia replied. "We're here to visit with whoever needs us."

The gentleman with them came over and shook Patricia's hand. "I bet you wonder why I'm wearing this giant mask. I'm quite allergic to dogs, though I've always loved animals. Before we got married, Mam had to put all the critters they used to have in the basement when I'd come to visit. I felt awful as I knew her pets were her passion. But she told me I was the only person she would ever *think* to put the animals away for and only because she liked me so much, and only because I am seriously allergic. This mask is making this visit bearable though. I've already sneezed through the tour as the cat was out and about. I can handle the dog. She's lovely by the way."

"Well, thank you, I certainly think so."

To make conversation she asked, "So, uh, how long has your mother been a resident at this facility?"

Peach realized she had no idea how to relate to elderly people. Her parents were in their eighties but they were active, alert, and lived in a lovely retirement community in Boulder. This woman was in a wheelchair, slumped over and the fool she was, as confident as she had felt handling this dog, and as equipped as she felt from the past six months of training, she realized she had left out one very important aspect of this endeavor. The human one. Thankfully, as is often the case, as dogs are better at relating to humans than humans are, Poppy stepped in.

Poppy

I still wanted that meatloaf. But maybe even more than that, I wanted to get to know the old human in the chair. I whined and pulled at my leash until my human relented and gave me some more slack. I walked gingerly over to her and licked her hand.

"Poppy! You have to wait until she lets you!" my human scolded me. Oh silly mommy, I thought. She has no idea what this person needs. I knew she wasn't going to pet me. I knew she wasn't going to light up and say "good doggy" and bark to my human about how sweet I am. I knew she was going to sit there in the chair with the big wheels and stare out the same window she had been staring out at since we got here. I didn't care. I wanted to pet *her* and I knew somehow it would help. Maybe for dogs it's less about the response we want and more about what we sense we should do.

Melody

Flynn was better at talking to people than she was, so she sat back as they conversed about dogs, the weather, Ireland, Boulder, and God knows what else. She just stared at the dog. Melody had always had a complicated relationship with dogs. On one hand, she always loved them as well as the many cats Mom had brought home over the years. But on the other hand, she constantly felt like she was vying for her mother's attention and the damn pets always got the best part of Mom, and she was always left with the rest. Now she was here with Mom in this facility, and she had not said a word since the day she got here. Melody was not a doctor but she could not imagine a person declining so rapidly in such a short time. The nurses said that if she didn't start eating soon they would have to start feeding her intravenously. She would occasionally drink some Ensure, if the nurses fed it to her with a straw, but besides that, her mother, who loved to cook and serve people and always took seconds was now refusing to eat. She looked at the dog. Maybe somehow this little creature could help Mom, because try as she may Melody herself sure could not.

Chapter Seven

Estelle

"Oh Clayton, you didn't have to do this!" she gushed, as she looked around the park. It was her 40th birthday and he had arranged a surprise party for her. All of her friends in rescue, including a few four legged ones, were all gathered at a picnic outside at their favorite park. He had said he was going to take her on a picnic for her birthday which wasn't untrue, however never would she have expected him to arrange something so wonderful, so meaningful to her. But then again she should not have been surprised. The festivities were so perfectly meant for her. She drank wine, petted dogs, and schmoozed with friends and acquaintances alike in the rescue community. A July birthday had the advantage of outdoor celebration, unlike Melody's birthday. Not much you could do on December 20th except look outside at the snow. Melody. Where was she? She looked over and saw her daughter petting Bella the collie, looking sad. Why on earth was she sad? Estelle wondered. She was around all of these wonderful dogs. She wished she understood her daughter, the bookish melancholy girl. The older she got, the more complicated she was becoming. Mr. Jones, their beagle came up to her and she petted his orange and black head and sighed. Dogs were so beautifully uncomplicated, while humans were incredibly so. Especially Estelle herself, as how on earth could she love everything about her life except for the thing she was supposed to love the most? Motherhood.

Estelle woke up to the hum of a machine attached to her bed. Where the hell was she? She looked over for Clayton. He was gone and this wasn't her bed. She touched her abdomen. It was raw and wrinkled and there was a tube inserted just above her navel. She did the only thing she knew to do. She began to scream. She screamed her daughter's name only in her confusion it sounded like

Ebony. Ebony? Where had she heard that name before? She kept trying to say Melody but the word came out wrong. Suddenly someone rushed to her side. She didn't know this person. She wanted her daughter, needed her right now. But she wasn't there, and in her place was a stranger.

"Mrs. Clayton, calm down, it's ok. What do you need?"

"Ebody, Ebony!" She screamed.

"Ebody? Who is Ebony?" After repeating the name another ten times she finally got the correct name. "Not Ebony goddammit, MELODY. I need Melody!"

Melody

She was getting ready for work, trying to straighten out her unruly hair when her phone rang. "That's funny" she thought, who would be calling this early? She looked at her phone. It was Sunshine Estates. She swallowed. She didn't want to answer the phone because it couldn't be good news, but she needed to get out of the habit of letting her phone go to voicemail. The voice message couldn't be any less foreboding than speaking to the nurse in person.

"Hello?"

"Mrs, Malley?"

"This is her."

"Hi, this is Abby, one of Mrs. Clayton's nurses. I just wanted to let you know that we have good news and bad news."

"Give me the bad news first."

"Well, it seems that she had a nightmare. She awoke very distraught and she was calling your name. In fact at first, she was calling 'Ebony' a name we didn't recognize. But finally she began to yell 'Melody'. So the bad news is that she woke up very agitated and her heart rate was elevated for some time, though it eventually slowed. However, this is literally the first time that she has spoken since she came here. After she settled down she refrained from speaking again and nightmares can cause people to yell in their sleep. But she knows who you are. Perhaps she got your name confused with a similar sounding name but it's a start. I know you have to get to work, but she did ask for you. Is there any chance you can come by tonight? After work?"

"Of course."

After hanging up, she sighed. Flynn had a thing to go to after work, and she figured this might be a good time to visit her mom without him. Melody knew that her mother's decline was partially physical; however, it would be foolish for her to ignore the fact that she and her mother had a long and complicated history.

After work Melody pulled her vehicle into the furthest parking space she could find. She wanted to take as long as she could to walk from her car to her mother's side, at Sunshine Estates. The day was cold and bitter, though there had been bright sun earlier. As she walked the sun faded, as if the universe was giving her an inkling of the conversation she was about to have with her mother's nurse. Melody wouldn't have been surprised if she heard foreboding movie music in the background.

Abby, the nurse that had called her that morning greeted her as she approached the front desk. "Hello Mrs. Malley."

"How is my mother?"

"Not much has changed since this morning, no more words but since Mrs. Clayton hasn't spoken since she arrived here we found her outburst rather significant. By the way, do you know of anyone named Ebony? I'm asking because in the beginning that was the name she was calling for. We figured it was just because she was confused and couldn't quite recall your name, but I thought I'd ask."

"Nope, not that I'm aware of. Maybe it was an old friend from before I was born. It could even have been the name of a pet. Mom had so many."

Abby smiled. "I see. Well, she's right this way but you already know that. Take all the time you wish. Visiting hours technically end at 8, but I won't rat you out if you stay later, I promise." Melody smiled. Her mother's condition seemed to be deteriorating in this place but she couldn't imagine it was because of the lack of compassion from the staff. Everyone she had met so far had been more than kind to her and her mother. So kind in fact, that Melody felt guilty. If they all knew how fucked up her family was they may not have been so kind. Ever since dad passed away the true dynamics of her family had begun to show the broken pottery that was her and her mother's relationship.

She entered the room and knocked on the door, entering as she did so. Before Estelle was put in this place, before dad died, before Melody was grown she always found herself knocking on her mother's door, always hesitant to request her attention. She marveled at the fact that she could jump into her father's arms, all the while feeling compelled to merely tiptoe into her mother's room, afraid, like she was in a museum and if she made too much noise, she would be removed.

"Mom?" Nothing.

"Mom, Abby called this morning. One of your nurses? She said you were asking for me. Ok first you were asking for someone named Ebony but then you asked for me. I had to go to work when she called but I'm here now. Is there something you want to say to me?"

She meant it as an invitation but it came out more like a challenge. Still, nothing. Was the nurse pulling her leg? Did she think she and Flynn didn't visit enough and this was her ploy to make her come more often? She didn't think so, as they didn't appear the least bit devious and everyone here seemed to genuinely like her and Flynn. "Mom, you can talk to me if you want. I don't mean to sound like I know more than the doctors but I think you know more than you let on. Though I can't believe you didn't pet the dog when it came in here last weekend. Anyway, I'm not sure what to say. I never know what to say. It seems like nothing I say is ever enough. Or anything I do is ever enough. Sometimes, I feel like I'm invisible to you. Like if I wasn't Dad, or one of your precious pets, or one of your friends, I was nobody. Like you didn't want some quiet studious girl. You wanted a mini version of yourself, and you didn't get that. And I'm sorry. I don't know what else to say. "Her voice filled with tears. "I'm not bold. I'm not outspoken...I'm not an advocate like you were, like you are. I can't talk to people like you did, I can't arrange lavish fundraisers. I can't get up on stage and thank the audience and talk to them and make them laugh like you did. I can't fight like you, or charm people like you, or convince people like you. I'm sorry, Mom. Sometimes I feel like you and Dad picked me out of the goddamn cabbage patch and I wasn't what you wanted and maybe you should have put me back."

At that point Melody could barely talk because her voice was so choked with tears. She looked at the clock on the wall—7:30. She didn't want to leave. But she needed a break. So she left and took a seat on one of the couches and let her tears fall freely.

Mac

So there I was, sitting on the couch licking my butt like I do every day at this hour and this human sat down. Usually the humans around here are so busy they don't have a minute for a catnap but this one sat right down next to me. I looked at her. I know people think us cats don't care about nothing but that's not true. We don't care about much, but we do care. I care about my coat and how shiny it is, getting the best spot on the rug to nap in the sun, and yeah, even a human every now and then. This one looked sad. Her eyes had water in them and she was shaking a little, but not like a purr, more like a cry. Humans are a weird bunch. They try to hide their cries. Once this fat guy stepped on my tail and you shoulda heard me! You probably did. I let out a yowl like you wouldn't believe! For the next ten minutes I hissed at anything I could see! The humans kept cooing, "oh, poor kitty, are you ok kitty?" No, I wasn't ok! My beautiful tail was ruined. Don't they know how vain cats are? Guess not, but this human was sitting there all sad so I did what I was there for. I postponed licking the rest of my butt and got in her face. I began to purr and rubbed my head against her hand. If that cuteness act didn't do it for her she must really be in a bad way.

"Hey" I chirped, you ok there? I'm Mac, I'm kind of King of this Castle. I'm here to cheer people up. All you gotta do is look at me and you'll feel better." Nothing. I climbed in her lap. She didn't stop me so that was a good sign. She petted my head and I purred. This was what she needed, much better than that dumb mutt who was here this afternoon. I don't know who let her in but if you're feeling blue you don't need no stinky dog, you need a beautiful refined feline to cheer you up. Since subtlety isn't one of my strengths, and

I'm as vain as a dog is clumsy, I soaked in her attention. I got in her face and as my whiskers tickled her cheek I saw a smile. She meowed to me in her language and while I don't speak human she sounded happier. Well duh, she got to meet the magic that is Mac the tabby, the most handsome fella in this joint. That'd make anyone purr down to their toes!

Melody

She petted the sweet little cat and he made her feel better, though little wasn't exactly the word she would use to describe him. It seemed he got quite a few table scraps from the residents here and she was sure the staff as well. This place seemed to have a surplus of pets around which seemed like it would be good for Mom, though her mother had taken no interest in her surroundings since her arrival.

Speaking to her mother back there had been cathartic. She didn't feel guilty. She felt like the things she said to her were not meant to offend but to get 45 years of rejection off her chest. Only who knew if her mother really understood what she had said? Melody had read up on a condition called catatonia—an almost trance like existence that sometimes manifested after a shock. But she couldn't deny the sudden and rapid decline in memory that her mother had faced these past few months either.

Melody shrugged. Maybe it was a combination of both? She'd never stopped loving her mother, but she'd never understood her either. They were two different people, but if Estelle had any chance at either regaining back what she once had, or in the very least, slow the progression of whatever this was down, she needed a way to connect with her. But how could she do that when she'd never been able to connect with her when she was healthy?

Chapter Eight

Peach

Her phone rang and she looked at the number. "Ugh." She knew it was his lawyer trying to set up a court date. She didn't want to. She didn't care. She would sign any paper he forwarded her but she had no desire to meet with him and discuss who gets what because she didn't want anything. He could have his oversized home to match his oversized ego. That house held terrible memories for her. She was a different person when she entered those heavy mahogany doors. She was Patricia, not Peach. She was a complacent wife to a powerful and dominating man. Before him and after him Peach was a woman who did what she wanted. Maybe she didn't always have the best sense of direction but even when she got lost, she had the confidence to find her way back again. Her whole life she had teetered on the brink of fear and confidence and this time, in this season in her life she was going to choose confidence no matter what the cost.

She let it go to voicemail and did the one thing she had not done since she left Sebastian six months ago. She called him.

"Hello? Patricia, Goddamit! Answer Ajay when he calls you next time! I want to get this over with. I don't have time to keep dealing with you. I don't want to give the house up, but since you were married to me for twenty-one years, Ajay *insisted* that I contact you." She could hear his eyes roll as he spoke. Maybe because every time he spoke to her in person his eyes rolled so far back in his head it looked like he was having a seizure.

"Sebastian, I don't care. I don't want anything. I don't want the house, or the money, or anything. All I want to do is part peacefully and not see you again."

"GOOD. And by the way you owe me $500 for the food you ate when you broke in before Thanksgiving. I accept cash, credit,

PayPal or Venmo. I won't even charge interest. Unless you're offering."

"Not anymore." She replied.

"Darn."

"Sebastian, why are you demanding money from me when I literally just told you that I don't want my share of your fortune. Can't we just call it even?"

"Since you were being so generous by forfeiting your rights to the money that I worked my ass off for, I thought maybe you wanted to reimburse me for your post-menopausal tirade after you left the best thing that's ever happened to you."

She hung up. Nothing like a fruitless conversation with the only person in human history that has ever had an effect on her gag reflex. Oy! But she knew she had to call Ajay at some point. Her husband's lawyer was as big of a prick as he was, but even he knew what was owed to her. She also knew any self-respecting individual would demand at least half of what was owed to them. But today was Sunday, and while those workaholics didn't care what day it was, *She* was going to wait until Monday to deal with any of it.

She had rented a small condo a few miles away from Pamela and the women got together often to catch up and of course play with Poppy. Peach had met many amazing residents at Sunshine Estates and everyone who met them loved Poppy.

There was one family in particular that bothered her though. The family with the woman who supposedly had Alzheimer's. The husband was friendly enough, the older woman said nothing, which was to be expected but it was the daughter who bothered her the most. She sat quietly and smiled at Poppy but never attempted to pet her, though she could tell that she wanted to. She could sense a disconnect between the mother and daughter, and while she knew the residents affairs were none of her business, her curiosity over the dynamics of this family intrigued her, nonetheless. Plus, Poppy was always pulling her into that room, and the cat was always wandering in there too, it was like the animals knew something the humans didn't.

Poppy

Dogs don't dream about the things that bother them. We dream about bones, bugs, birds, bacon, rabbits, bacon, kibble, playing fetch, and bacon. I still dream about those meatballs though they almost cost me my life. But every time mom takes me to that place that smells like potatoes and pot roast something bothers me. It's this one room, the one with the guy with the muzzle and the lady in the wheelchair. They seem sad. A lot of people here seem sad, but when they see me they perk right up. Who wouldn't? I've looked in the mirror. Teddy was right. No wonder people love us. So here we were, walking through the hall, and that brat hissed at me again. Ugh, what did he want?

"Yo, mutt." I turned around.

"Really?"

"No, listen up, I got some advice for you."

"Yeah?"

"That room, the one with the guy with the muzzle and the two females. Go for the young female first. Don't go for the male, your fur might kill him. But pet the youngest female. Trust me, she needs you. Well, she needs me but I guess a dirty mutt will do."

"Thanks, bratty fat cat," I replied, but smiled as I did.

Mom wanted to visit the old couple who fed me Cheetos first, and as much as I could eat Cheetos all day, I insisted we go to the room with the lady in the wheelchair. I whined and pulled until she relented, because I knew she always would. Six months of "training" and I still get my way, who pays these people?

Peach

Her dog was obsessed with room 107. In all honesty so was she. By some stroke of luck, the woman's family was always there whenever she visited. She figured it was because Saturdays were when most families visited the residents. She knocked on the door.

"Helloo. It's Peach and Poppy, mind if we come in and say 'hello'? Poppy really wants to!"

"Come in." said the only person in the room who should be avoiding the dogs, but the only one who ever answered.

"How is everyone today? How are you feeling, Mrs. Clayton?" As usual the woman didn't answer and her son-in-law gave a glib response, ignorant, but to the best of his ability, as his mother-in-law wouldn't speak. His wife, as usual said nothing. Poppy pulled to where she was sitting and began to whine. "Poppy, you have to *ask* to be petted" she reminded her gently.

"It's ok," the woman replied, the first words she had spoken, really since Peach had begun visiting them. She pet the dog's head gingerly. Poppy continued to rub her head against the woman's hand, almost like a cat, if she could believe that.

Melody

This woman and her dog always came into visit. The dog seemed to really take a liking to her, though her mother was always the dog person. She thought maybe the Alzheimer's had made her mom lose her dog vibe but she couldn't believe that, even if this evil disease did take away so much.

She looked at the woman with the dog. "Peach". What a name. She seemed so vibrant and eccentric, and dressed in bright colors, floral skirts, knitted sweaters, and colorful jewelry. She seemed so confident and happy and Melody wondered what her secret was. So, she did one of the ballsiest things she had done in a long time. She motioned to the lady and asked if she could speak to her in the hall. This was partially because she could see Flynn's eyes well up from dog dander in spite of the mask he wore, and also because her mother had fallen asleep and she needed to get out of that room.

She'd of course spoken to Flynn about her encounter with mom Monday evening, and while as usual he listened sympathetically, he had nothing to really offer other than maybe Mom had had a nightmare and wanted to see her, which was, duh, exactly what happened. But why? There was something about Peach, something she could trust even though they were virtual strangers. The woman probably thought she was a bitch because the past three times she had visited them she had said virtually nothing to her, and now she was asking her advice. The woman with her perfect eyebrows, no doubt highlighted professionally, looked at her with interest.

"What can I do for you?"

"I know you're not a doctor, or a nurse, or even a psychologist, but the truth is that's why I wanted to talk to you. You see, my mom and I have been estranged. My father passed away over a year ago and since he died, my husband and I haven't visit her as much as we could have, and of course she took his death really hard. She was madly in love with my father, and his illness, and eventual passing really broke her. I think, the way she used to be, reminds me a bit of you. Of course I don't know you, it's just that believe it or not, she was once a dog person too. She worked in animal rescue. She was amazing. She trained dogs. She ran these fundraisers, everything. But right before she moved here she was diagnosed with Alzheimer's."

Peach nodded. She seemed to understand. "I see. She sounds amazing. Heck, it seems like she'd run circles around me in her younger days!"

"You? Really? It seems like you do so much. Wow, I know I don't know you well, and I know it seems like I've not been paying attention, but I have. I guess that's one of the things about me that Mom got wrong. It may have seemed like I wasn't paying attention but I was. I am. I guess, sadly I'd not been paying much attention these past few months, or else I would have noticed mom's decline. I could blame anyone else, my husband, my mom's friends, her doctor, the clergy who promised to check up on her, and probably didn't or even mom herself for not calling and saying 'Help, Mel, I'm losing it!' but the truth is I have no one to blame but myself."

Peach motioned for her to come over to the couch and sit down and as they did the dog sat next to her. The tabby cat was on top of the couch backrest and for some reason, when he saw the dog, he didn't bolt. The dog didn't make a sound either. She was surprised.

"I'd want to blame anyone else too for the predicament I was in for the past twenty-one years but the truth is for this I also have no one to blame but myself." Peach said.

"For what?"

"Well, you spilled to me, so I guess I'll spill to you too. You know, when I got this little Poppy dog I was so excited about getting her trained to go and make a difference and we did. The trainers and myself did a fine job helping this girl be ready to go into the world and cheer people up! But this old girl?" she said, pointing to herself, chuckling, "was an old dog who needed some new tricks. You see I was married to this tyrant for twenty-one years and before that I dated him for five. My ex, and goddamn that feels good to refer to him as such, was wealthy and successful. Successful at making everyone around him feel like shit. I chose to stick with him because deep down, I didn't think I could do better. I found this little gal in a parking lot. I took her home to the hubs and he said 'no way! If you keep her I'll divorce you.' I replied, 'ok, you do that.' It's like this skinny little stray finally gave me the courage to do something that I should have done a long time ago.

"Speaking of dogs, our neighbor's dog hated him. That should have been a red flag, huh? Pets seem to really like your mom. I believe pets can read people very well, far better than we can read one another, it seems. My dog seems pretty obsessed with your mom. Like she can tell that deep down she's a dog person. Then you got that cat over there slinking his fat body around her wheelchair all day!"

"He probably wants her lunch and dinner.."

"Probably. But he seems pretty affectionate for a kitty. But anyways, here I am, it's been a wild six months and I have a long way to go. I'm a hot mess, but I'm upright and my life has purpose. And by the way, Melody, if you truly feel like your mother was misdiagnosed, I would advise you to talk to the doctor. While she seems catatonic, to me it doesn't mean Alzheimer's is her final diagnosis. I'm not a doctor, but neither are you and if I were you I'd seek a second opinion."

Poppy

The old tabby was sitting on the couch looking stoic as usual. His eyes blinked slowly, which is what I do when I'm happy. He was either happy or constipated but as he sat the humans talked. And talked and talked. I had no idea what anyone was saying but as I closed my eyes dreaming that one of those nice nurses would fix me a plate of pot roast the cat hissed again. Really? Can't a dog dream around here?

"What?"

"Your human's nice."

"I know."

"She slips me pieces of fish sometimes."

"Big deal, she gives me steak."

"I think the old human in the chair is awake now."

"What's your point?"

"Make your human go into the room. Oh wait, I forgot, you're not a cat. Nobody listens to you."

"Yes she does!" I barked.

"Shhh, Poppy!" my mom said.

"Case in point. One point for the cat. Well, when they go back in there, sit next to the old human."

"Duh, I was going to, furball."

"Don't screw it up, fleabag. For some reason I can't explain, as much as the old lady likes cats she likes dogs even better. Had a bunch of em before she came to this joint."

"How do you know?"

"I'm quasi-fluent in human. Impressed?"

"No."

"You're bluffing."

"If you're so smart, you'd know whether I am or not. Meanwhile, she likes dogs better, so one point for the dog. Enjoy your tuna, hairball. I'm getting steak." I bragged as I finally followed my human back into the room.

The old lady and I had one thing in common. Neither of us had any idea what anyone in the room was saying. Unlike the braggy tabby I didn't pay attention in English class. Darn. But I was born with charm as all dogs are. So I did the thing. I put my head on her lap, I nosed her hand. I avoided her untouched lunch though I wanted to finish it. Nothing. I sighed and it came out in a frustrated huff. Finally, I looked at her. She didn't look at me, but I told her, in my own way "I know what it's like to be lost. I was lost for a long time. But it's ok. You'll be found one day, I promise. And when you are, you won't ever look back." I felt a hand on my head. Was it my human? No, it was her, just a brush of her thumb on my forehead. But it was enough. Enough to know she heard me.

Melody

Melody couldn't stop thinking about her conversation with Peach. She was completely shocked that she'd been in a bad marriage. She seemed so confident, and competent, so together.

She told Flynn about Peach and he responded, "Why are you so surprised?"

"It's just that she seemed so, well, sophisticated and successful."

"Can't sophisticated and successful people break sometimes?"

"Well, sure."

"Like your mam."

"Mom?"

"Yes, Melody, your mom. I know you think she was some sort of hero whom you could never measure up to, but right now she's in a nursing home pissing in Depends so maybe, just maybe she's not as impossible to live up to as you once thought she was!"

"Where is all this coming from?"

"Oh, I don't know, Melody. I guess I'm just tired of you having a hero complex. Like maybe the woman I married isn't below everyone she meets! Like maybe, when I met you, and fell in love with you, I wasn't wrong about you. Because I think you're pretty damn amazing Melody Lynne but sometimes you're too fucking blind to see that yourself!"

"I'm sorry..."

"Don't be sorry. Love yourself. Love yourself enough to FIGHT for the things you believe to be true. There is too much inside of you to keep stuffing down into your gut. It's not fair to you. I know you believe mam may not have Alzheimer's but you're too afraid of her doctor to confront him or to even seek a second opinion. And now, Mam's sitting there in a wheelchair, maybe not receiving the treatment she really *needs* all because her daughter is just letting things go, because you're too afraid. And the truth is I could talk to the doctor. I want to, but you need to." His voice softened then. "I'm saying this because I love you. Because I believe in you. You're not inferior to your mother. You're not inferior to the lady with the dog. You're not *inferior* to anyone. You are worthy, Mel and every night my prayer is that you would begin to believe that.

They were lying in bed that night and Melody rolled over and mumbled "Just because someone is quiet doesn't mean they don't have opinions."

"I know you have opinions," Flynn replied. "I like when you express them. It kind of turns me on!"

"Goodnight Flynn. And thanks, that's a good incentive."

Chapter Nine

Estelle

She was walking and walking and couldn't find her way home. She looked one way looking for Stuart, the other looking for Melody. She saw neither and in front of her, she frantically looked for a dog. She knew, somehow, that most of the time, when she was walking, there was a dog of one type or another in front of her. Now there was nothing--no family, no dog, nothing. She looked at her hands. They were old and wrinkled, surely not her own. What was happening? Where was she? She opened her eyes and saw that she was not walking at all. In fact she was sitting down, and someone was pushing her. Pushing her? Where? And how? She looked at her feet. They were placed on two foot rests and her arms were on two arm rests. Where was she going? She felt two hands lift her and place her onto a cold, metal table. Frightened, she wanted to scream, to fight, to tell them to keep their paws off her, dammit, but she was tired. So tired. So she closed her eyes. And that uncomfortable metal table became the bed which she fell asleep on.

Melody

"Mr. and Mrs. Malley, the results are back in from your mother's most recent MRI." Dr. Anders sat across a large mahogany table, his hands folded in front of him. "I'm afraid the results are the exact same as the scan we did six months ago, indicating advanced Alzheimer's. The good news is that the buildup of beta amyloid has not increased any, which is really quite surprising due to her rapid decline."

Flynn raised his hand halfway, looked at his wife, sighed, and continued with the question he knew they both had. "Dr. Anders, if the buildup of beta amyloid hasn't increased any in these past six months, even though she has been declining rapidly, do you think that Alzheimer's is the only conclusion that can be drawn based on her symptoms?"

The doctor looked at him and raised an eyebrow. "Are you suggesting that our conclusion is incorrect?"

"Well..."

"She has every symptom. Despondency, inability to recognize familiar people, increased sleep, decreased mobility; the list goes on! Mr. Malley, if you're suggesting that my findings are incorrect then you are welcome to seek a second opinion, but in my opinion, you're both wasting your time."

"Well, my mother is wasting away."

"Excuse me, Mrs. Malley?"

It's been said before. Bullies like to play chess. They block you in on all four sides and you are in such a quandary that you have no choice left but to surrender. The only way out is to change the name of the game. A game where you actually have a chance of winning, because for the first time, you are given a chance. For the first time in her life, Melody changed the name of the game, and the game was one where she would be making the rules.

"My mother is wasting away. And I don't like it."

"Mrs. Malley with all due respect..."

Melody put a hand up. "I'm not finished. My mother isn't being treated. The staff at Sunshine Estate are taking excellent care of her but there is only so much they can do. And if her diagnosis is incorrect, then there is no way to know *how* to treat her. You've not put her on any medication, suggested any cognitive rehabilitation therapy, etc. You simply told me she has Alzheimer's and your *nurse* gave us a list of nursing homes. Like that's it. Like a woman who has literally given her whole life to love and serve others is just being put into a home to die, and sit there until she does. It's not right. And yes, Dr. Anders, to answer your question, we *would* like a second opinion."

Melody was shaking when she left the office that afternoon. She reached for Flynn's hand, as he embraced hers she felt his wedding ring, hard and metallic against her fingers. There was no way she could have said what she did back there without him by her side.

"You were amazing, love." Flynn said.

"I couldn't have done it without you." Melody replied.

"You couldn't have done it without her."

"Who?"

"Your Mam."

She sighed. He wasn't wrong. Melody put her hand to her heart. She knew, somewhere deep within it, hidden was her mother's DNA, the fighter, the advocate, the warrior. Melody had been wrong. Strength isn't a personality trait. It's intrinsic in every human being and it is manifested in different ways in different people at different times.

"Melody, if you don't think Mam has Alzheimer's what do you propose she has? I'm not challenging your opinion, I think maybe there's something else going on too. However, I can't imagine what it is."

"I can't either, but I know Mom has been depressed since Dad passed away and I know her family and community have not been the most supportive. I think she has some memory loss as most people her age have anyway, and she could have a touch of dementia but I think, at least based on what I've seen in other people, Alzheimer's is usually different. Like people have spells. Like they're super lucid then all the sudden they don't know who you are, or who they are for that matter. Yes, they get crabby too, but part of that is because they are losing themselves. I truly think Dr. Anders saw what he saw and ran with it because it was the easiest diagnosis. But it wasn't the only conclusion he could have drawn. If he had actually VISITED her more than twice since November, he would have a better idea of what he was dealing with. Sending a nurse to do a five minute visit, checking her vitals, and confirming with the care staff that she's still not eating, and still being fed through a tube does not count as a visit."

"That pissed me off too," agreed Flynn. "Sending a nurse is not the same thing as visiting her yourself. She's HIS patient! Not the nurse's. It feels like she's more his problem, and we're a bother to him. I feel like some doctors deal with patients because they want to maintain their reputation as a doctor, but when they actually have patients they visit them as little as possible and do the least they can just to squeak by so they can maintain their status."

"I agree. But for now, we need to find a new doctor in her network, because I don't think I can look at Dr. Anders' smug face for one more visit without sucker punching it!"

"That's the feisty girl I know!"

Flynn and Melody were sitting with Estelle on a Sunday afternoon. All was quiet, and because it was a Sunday they couldn't commence their search for a new doctor. So they took the afternoon to visit, and look for subtle signs of either change in a positive way or even more decline, though it seemed like the past four months or so have been more of the same every day. Estelle dosing in her wheelchair while Melody read a book and Flynn did the New York Times crossword puzzle on his laptop. It was so quiet in the room. All that could be heard was the hum of the patient's machine next door, the sound of medicine carts rolling by, and the occasional sniffle from Flynn as his mask didn't completely protect his sinuses from the cat's fur. All of a sudden Estelle raised her head. She began to mumble something. One word, very quietly. Melody put her book down and walked over to her mother's side. "Mom? What are you trying to say?" She was afraid that her overenthusiasm would scare her mother from repeating what she wanted to say, but she couldn't help herself. With the exception of her outburst a few months ago, her mother hadn't spoken since November.

Estelle repeated herself. "Poppy. Poppy?"

"What's she saying?" Flynn looked up.

"She's asking for Poppy."

"Who the hell is Poppy?"

"I don't know. A nurse maybe?"

"Maybe. Do you think we should ask one of the staff if they know a Poppy who works here?"

"Couldn't hurt. I wouldn't be surprised if it was a dog she used to take care of. But nonetheless she said something! It's a miracle. A small miracle, but it's something."

Peach had given Melody her phone number in case she wanted to talk. Melody didn't feel comfortable using it as she barely knew her, so had not up to this moment, but felt that this moment was newsworthy as Peach had grown quite fond of Estelle.

"Hi Peach, I just wanted to let you know that my mom actually spoke today. One word but still significant. She said "Poppy" and we have no idea who that is but we're happy for this progress. Flynn is speaking to the nurses now to ask who that might be."

Five minutes later, Peach responded with ten laughing emojis. A second later her name showed up on a phone call. Melody answered it, confused.

"Hi, Peach?"

When she finally stopped laughing and was able to compose herself, she sputtered out, "Melody! Poppy is my *dog*! She was asking about the dog!"

"Oh, how *funny*! Since my mother's diagnosis and move to Sunshine Estate she has spoken two words. First my name, then said nothing else once I came to visit her, probably because I basically told her off, and now, she asked about the dog! Of course she did. Never mind Flynn, myself, you or the myriad of nurses who are catering to her night and day, but the dog. Some things never change."

Melody could almost hear Peach smile over the phone. "Melody, that means your mother is still in there somewhere, you know? Like she hasn't completely lost who she is. And for the record I think that doctor of hers is a quack. He gave her this diagnosis, stuck her in a home, and never bothered to come check up on her. Trust me, I can smell rotten from a mile away; I was married to it for twenty-one years. So I *just* got back from a friend's wedding so we weren't able to make it up this weekend, because the wedding was in Boulder, which is just as gorgeous as I remember, by the way, but next Saturday I'm planning on bringing Poppy over. Will you two be there?"

"We were planning on Sunday again, but can definitely switch it to Saturday.

"Great, and Melody? Don't give up on your mom. I have a feeling she wants to get better but she needs you to fight for her. Don't stop. Because I know you can help her. You and my sweet little dog."

Chapter Ten

Peach

Once she hung up with Melody and got home from the wedding she opened her mail. In the middle of the envelopes was a subpoena for court. "He'd better not be suing me for any of my money, I hardly have any, and God knows he won't willingly hand over a penny of his fortune to me." Just then her email buzzed and she opened the latest message, one from her husband's lawyer. It read,

"Dear Ms. Rueben,

I am writing to advise you to appear in court next Wednesday. I understand the temptation to opt out however, and you did not hear this from me, but Mr. Garret is obligated to divide his funds in half, given the length of time you were married. If you do not appear in court, he keeps it all. If you do, you will have access to what is rightfully yours.

Sincerely,

Ajay Vindhu"

She read it over three times to make sure she was reading right. Why on earth would a man who was being paid to make sure that his client wins give his opponent a tip to come and claim what is theirs? Unless he felt the same way about Sebastian that the rest of the world felt about him. She stifled a laugh. Maybe Mr. Vindhu wasn't such a bad guy after all. She was so incredibly tempted to prove to herself and to the rest of the world that she didn't need his money. That she could go on living a perfectly happy and simple life with her dog, doing odd jobs and barely qualifying for health insurance. What was the point in that, and what was she trying to prove? She knew Ajay was embellishing and that there was no way that she was entitled to half of his money but whatever she won would be a pretty penny, and there was no limit to what she could do with it. Her mind began to reel with the many possibilities of what that money could buy. She looked at Poppy at her feet. She could certainly make a sizable donation to the Humane Association in Denver. She could put a lot of it into savings and donate a lot to various charities including the Denver Indian center, an organization close to her heart. Before she met Sebastian she was pursuing a degree in Native American studies. Once she met him she dropped out of school to help him follow his dreams. She had sacrificed and lost so much by marrying him, and now, it was her turn to receive some of it back, and she intended to use it to invest in the things she was passionate about.

She discussed the lawyer's letter with Pamela. "Peach, there are so many things you can use this money for, but neither of us are holding our breath for him to give you a cent more than he's obligated. But y'all were married for twenty-one years and you put up with him longer than that. He owes you! The universe owes you. You've put up with so much these past twenty years, and even more so in these recent years. Being stuck in a house with an abusive person during a pandemic wasn't easy. You deserve so much more. I know this is the LPC in me rearing its head but I guess I can't help myself. I've held onto a lot of righteous anger in regards to your situation for a long time, and now that this opportunity has been put before you, I urge you to milk it for all it's worth. You need to get yourself a lawyer and fight like hell. "

She knew Pamela was right. She had sold herself in order to fulfill a dream she thought she'd always had, but the truth was it was a dream that other people had had for her that she obediently went along with. The whole time she was married to Sebastian there was this feral bitch inside of her screaming to get out and ironically it took a feral bitch of the canine species for her to recognize this. She smiled at her dog. Looking at her she saw not just one pit bull but every single pit bull in the greater Denver area. If she did win this settlement, she knew exactly what she would do with it.

Chapter Eleven

Melody

Estelle hadn't spoken a single word after inquiring about Poppy that Sunday afternoon. She had, however, with prompting, taken a few bites of food. When the cat came into the room she would smile, if just for a moment.

Melody was in her mom's room one Saturday morning on her phone looking for a doctor to replace Dr. Anders. There were a lot of doctors in her mother's network who took Medicare, so the decision wasn't easy. She and Flynn had not even begun to contact physicians, as the day after Estelle had spoken and the few days after they basically told Dr. Anders that he was fired had been busy for both of them at work. They had taken turns visiting Estelle after work in hopes that she would speak again, though to no avail.

However, after that day something had shifted between Melody and her mother. It had seemed like in the past, whenever Melody entered her mother's room, she had the same foreboding feeling that she'd had as a child when she approached her mother. The feeling that she was intruding. However, after the day she spoke, something in Melody had changed, a confidence ensued and it had affected the way she felt and in turn it seemed to affect Estelle's demeanor as well. While she spoke and ate as little as she had in the past few months, there was a calm that was undeniable. It had manifested physically as well, as her blood pressure and heart rate had decreased bringing them down to a healthier level. However, the staff at the nursing home could only do so much to help Estelle. She needed a doctor as well as a team of staff to continue to evaluate her progress or lack thereof and see what more could be done to help her.

Melody was scrolling down her phone when she saw a picture of a young female doctor. What caught her attention was that this woman had a picture of herself with her dog! Dr. Vida Gamal. Flynn was sitting next to her in their living room, and she turned to show him her picture on her phone.

"Flynn, this one doctor really caught my eye. She put up a picture with her dog. "

Flynn began to laugh. "I was *just* going to show you her bio! She seems perfect. Of course one picture doesn't define a person, but I was getting a good vibe too. It seems like a dog has been the catalyst to Mam's *potential* improvement and to involve a doctor in her treatment that obviously loves dogs only makes sense."

First Melody and Flynn had an in person consultation with Dr. Gamal. She asked a series of very specific questions regarding her mother's care as well as the details surrounding her gradual decline, some of which, to her embarrassment, Melody was not able to answer. She expected the doctor to be appalled by this fact. She began to worry because she could not recall the exact moment of the onset of her mother's decline. Would the doctor have enough details to correctly diagnose her mother?

"I would like to arrange for Mrs. Clayton to be evaluated by a series of doctors including myself, along with a psychologist, and if necessary a physical and occupational therapist." Flynn raised a finger and Dr. Gamal smiled and nodded. "I realize that at this point she is not speaking. However, I think with the whole family together along with a psychologist some questions can be answered. Based solely on what I have been told, Mrs. Clayton could be suffering from Alzheimer's, however her MRI paired with the nurse's assessment of her current state do not add up. I will go and visit her on Friday morning and take it from there. All patients deserve a chance to receive the best possible care, and it grieves me that she has been stagnant in a nursing facility for the past seven months. But now is as good of time as any to change that. It was nice meeting you both today. After my assessment of her on Friday, I will contact you with the next step and the best approach to her treatment."

Estelle

Nothing made sense in this place. She was starving but could not eat, exhausted but could not sleep. She recalled every detail of her past life, but for the life of her could not tell you the time of day. She wanted to open her mouth and scream, but any time when she opened her mouth all she could do was gasp. She closed her eyes as her head slumped onto her chest for the millionth time since she found herself captive. Memories stung her, memories of Ebony then Melody, maybe not in that order, two girls, girls whom she had let down in one way or another. "I'm sorry" she would breathe, would gasp, but no words would come out. No tears would escape her, only the hidden shame that she had swallowed churned within her as each day bled into the next. She was hungry, wet, tired, and afraid but somewhere, deep within her she knew this was not her real life. She wasn't sure if she believed in a higher power, but just in case she did, she implored Them, whoever They were, to give her the strength to claw her way out of this abyss.

Melody

Dr. Gamal didn't get around to calling Melody until Monday afternoon. She was sitting outside on the bench next to the library when her phone buzzed. She picked it up and the moment she said hello and Dr. Gamal returned the greeting, she could hear a smile in her voice.

"Hello, Mrs. Malley. I was able to meet with your mother and talk with some of the nursing staff who have been responsible for her care these past few months. I have nothing but good things to say about these folks, and it seems as if your mother is in very good hands. Based on my initial observation, I think it would be advisable to compile a team of professionals to continue to assess your mother, and I am going to go ahead and email you a list of psychologists to choose from, for your whole family to speak with. The list contains ten doctors. However, I personally know each one, and any of them would be an asset to your family. It's more a matter of whom you prefer as well as what their availability is with your family's schedule. I've worked personally with all of them and have nothing but positive things to say. After speaking with them a couple of times, we will determine whether or not physical, occupational, and cognitive therapy will be needed as opposed to simply palliative care. Do you have any questions?"

"Do you think my mother will need palliative care, or is there hope for her improvement?" Melody asked.

"I certainly believe that Mrs. Clayton has the ability to improve and the quality of her improvement depends upon her willingness to do the work," Dr. Gamal replied.

Melody let out a breath and the doctor laughed. "I know it is a lot to take in, but this is all positive, Mrs. Malley. We have a long road ahead of us, but not a hopeless one, not in the least."

Poppy

I don't like storms. They remind me of my days as a stray when it was a gamble of whether or not I'd find shelter soon enough or get soaked to the bone, or worse yet get hit by that yellow stuff in the sky. Dog only knows what that loud stuff could do to a pup, probably smash us into a million furry pieces. I was in what was kind of becoming my happy place, the room with the old lady in the chair and the guy with the mask. I liked his female too, she still didn't say much but she was nice and beginning to warm up to me. But today was different because the sky was as gray as my coat and starting to make those funny sounds again, like a big truck getting closer and closer. I began to panic. But then something happened.

Peach

Peach knew that Poppy had a fear of storms and tried to avoid taking her anywhere when one was forecasted. Most people who met Poppy loved her, but there was always that stigma attached to pit bull terriers, and Peach did not like her spooking in public for that reason. However, this day advertised sunny skies until 6 p.m., and she'd taken Poppy to go visiting at Sunshine Estates at three. However the meteorologists were wrong, and darkness crept across the blue sky and thunder growled its foreboding sound. Poppy began to tremble, and sat on the floor with her legs out and head between her paws. She knew she'd better leave soon but suddenly something nobody expected happened.

Estelle took a piece of beef off of her untouched plate and looked at the dog. Without a word she motioned for her to come near. Poppy did, still trembling, and when the thunder boomed she put her empty hand on the dog's head. Once the noise stopped she patted her and offered her the beef, weakly in her other hand. Of course Poppy took it and gobbled it up, looking at her for more. The thunder subsided until it went for a second round, and Estelle repeated the trick with Poppy. The dog still seemed a bit uneasy over the weather but was much calmer than Peach had ever seen her in the middle of a storm. She was astonished. In the past four months that they had been visiting with Estelle, she had never seen her so much as move, let alone train a dog to tolerate thunder. She looked at the old woman, still, to some extent held hostage by her despondency. She knew that somehow, somewhere the old Mrs. Clayton was buried deep inside and today a part of her peeked out. Everyone in the room held onto the hope that they would see more of that version of her very soon.

Chapter Twelve

Melody

Back home Melody put her hand over her face, rubbing it in disbelief for the hundredth time. Flynn had the same expression on his face. "I'm completely astonished. It's not like Mom spoke or anything but the old dog trainer, the woman who probably saved hundreds of families from having to return their dogs to the shelter seemed to resurrect today. I know she knew exactly what she was doing. She did the exact same thing with Jackson, our rescued Rottie, when he was afraid of storms. Mom *always* kept ground beef in the fridge just in case she needed to teach one of our many dogs a new trick or help them overcome a fear. It never worked on any of the cats, though." she added with a laugh.

Flynn returned the laugh and added,

"Melody, I think Dr. Gamal has very good intuition. I think it will be a long road but today was a very good sign. Not only did Mam act like herself again but she actually helped the little dog overcome a fear, at least in that moment. Patricia said she would definitely try that trick the next time Poppy is afraid."

After much thought and research, Melody and Flynn decided on a psychologist. Dr. Gavin McIntyre had been practicing for the past forty years. He was set to retire soon and one of the reasons they chose him was the fact that he was only ten years younger than Estelle herself. While he obviously had his wits intact and was competent to practice medicine, Melody and Flynn liked the idea of a doctor who was a little on the older side. Plus, he was Scottish which Flynn admired.

Melody became increasingly nervous as their first appointment with Dr. McIntyre approached. She laughed as she envisioned her mother patting her head and putting a bit of ground beef to her lips. If only training a human was that easy.

Estelle was in her chair, half asleep, as Dr. McIntyre knocked and entered the room. He was a tall man with a head of thin white hair, a slight bald spot at the top of his head, as well as a thick white beard, making him look a bit like Santa Claus. He had a friendly demeanor and extended a long arm to shake both of their hands. He gently touched Estelle's arm and introduced himself to her as well. He spoke with the same confident tone to all three of the family members and got right down to business, smiling the whole time. Melody liked him, his presence was comforting and she hoped he could shed some light on what the next steps were to be.

"Mr. and Mrs. Malley, the first thing I want to do is ask both of you to describe what you knew of Mrs. Clayton before she entered Sunshine Estate. I'm sure you both have very different perceptions based on the length of time you have each known her, but it helps to get a feel of how each of you perceive her, as well as your relationship with her. I encourage you to be respectful but as honest as you can, leaving nothing out. The old adage about the truth setting us free still holds true."

Melody touched Flynn's arm. She wanted him to go first. It would give her time to think of exactly what to say.

Flynn began, "I have known Mrs. Clayton since 2010, when I met Melody. I want to start off by saying that when I first met Mrs. Clayton and her husband I liked them both right away, however, even if I had not liked them, nothing on earth would have prevented me from marrying their daughter. I am grateful to the Claytons because if not for them my wife wouldn't exist and I am truly, madly, and deeply in love with her. To be honest, I don't think either woman gives the other enough credit.

"I'll start with Mrs. Clayton. There were times when we were all together, especially while Mr. Clayton was still alive, when Mrs. Clayton would not look at Melody. I don't believe this was intentional, but I always got the impression that in Mrs. Clayton's eyes everything Mr. Clayton said was of the utmost importance while what Melody said was overlooked. Mr. Clayton would always hang onto every word either of us said. However when it was just Estelle with the two of us she would often act as if what Melody had to say was less important. Perhaps 'dismissive' is the word best used to describe it. Estelle has been nothing but kind to me since the day I met her. However, whenever I sang her daughter's praises, she often changed the subject. I don't think she sees what an amazing daughter she has, and I think my wife also overlooks her mother's merits. Mrs. Clayton is never mean to Melody as far as I can see. However, I don't believe she has ever been nice to her either. I admire Mrs. Clayton for many reasons, but a person can be the bee's knees but also, at the same time deeply flawed."

Dr. McIntyre nodded. "Thank you Mr. Malley. That was very helpful. It helps to have a somewhat impartial third party in any situation. Mrs. Malley, if it's ok, I would like to hear your experience with your mother now. Please, feel free to speak freely.

"Would it be ok if at first I spoke a little bit about my father to segue into Mom?"

"Of course, whatever feels the most comfortable for you."

"Thank you. I had a hard time with my father's illness and eventual death and I know Mom did too. It was hard to watch him suffer, and selfishly, my fears revolving around his illness and eventual passing were more that soon I would lose one of the only people in the world who ever understood me. I am fortunate enough to be married to the only other person who I believe understands me well." Melody stated, looking at her husband and smiling. "I was always what people call a 'daddy's girl.' I don't really like that title but I was attached to my father. We had a blast together. We would fish together, hike together. He loved nature and knew so much about the native fauna of Colorado. He was so colorful and brilliant and if I am half the woman that he was, I am happy. The truth is I can say the exact same thing about my mother with the exception of the first part. Mom is so admirable in so many ways. I'm not sure what you know about her and how she was before she began to lose her memory, but she was a powerhouse in the Denver Rescue Community. She has an amazing gift with dogs and has helped numerous families work with their new dog to make them a compatible pet so they won't have to make the terrible decision to return it to the shelter. I love animals but there have been so many times in my life that I have been resentful of them because it seemed like they took precedence over Mom's relationship with me. And of course I would feel guilty about that because it's not the animals fault. And the whole time all I wanted was for my mother to love me and she was over there in love with her work and I always hid in the shadows." There were tears in her voice and Flynn put an arm around her shoulder. She continued, drawing from his strength as well as the gnawing hunger within herself to somehow make her relationship with her mom right, before it was too late.

"I'm not like my mom. I'm not bold. I'm not a good speaker." She looked over and saw Flynn shaking his head. She knew he didn't agree with her but she continued anyway. "I think maybe in some ways she was disappointed that I am not more like her. That I didn't care about the things that were important to her. She's not wrong. I don't think it's my calling to go into animal rescue but it is my calling to love what I do and do it with passion and I feel like I'm not doing that and that disappoints her. I can't speak for my father anymore, but when he was alive he would support me in anything I pursued." She paused then and took a deep breath. "I think that above anything else he would love to see Mom and I reconcile."

Dr. McIntyre smiled. "Thank you, Melody and Flynn. This was all very helpful. Both of you are very articulate and insightful people." He smiled again. "I can see how you are so compatible." Flynn raised a finger.

"Yes?" asked the doctor.

"Do you think Mrs. Clayton heard anything we said today? Just based on your professional opinion."

"Only time will tell. I would like to continue to have more sessions like we did today. I think they give me helpful insight into the dynamics of this family and help all of you to heal. Maybe this is what Mrs. Clayton needs. To absorb some hard truths, but also to feel that spirit of love and forgiveness.

Chapter Thirteen

Peach

We have so many gods in our lives. So many false deities with false rules and deep rooted tyranny that we often have no idea they are holding us captive. We are like a frog who has no idea it is being boiled alive because it is so used to the heat. Captivity is dangerous. Revelation is even more dangerous to the capturer. Because finally their hostage realizes that there is a better life out there and that it is attainable once they take the first step. Blinders fall off and you realize you are more than who you have been for the past number of years. You get your old name back, your own personality and style. You finally get what was always yours. You will mourn what you lost and you may even take a moment to mourn the depravity of your narcissistic bully but then you will look forward. The journey is arduous but it is worth every step and you get to take each one wearing the clothing and image that is comfortable for you.

Patricia sat in the courtroom on that Thursday afternoon and once the conclusion was drawn by the judge and it was decided that Sebastian had to hand over half of his fortune to her, she began to feel faint. The room began to spin and finally, everything went dark.

When she came to, her head hurt and one of the security guards put his hand on her back and offered her small sips of water. She struggled to remember what had occurred before she apparently went out cold.

"What exactly happened?" She asked weakly, as she attempted to sit up. In the corner of her eye she saw Sebastian and as usual he looked constipated and was rolling his eyes. It all came back to her. She had won half that SOB's money. She rubbed her head and allowed the security guard to help her into a chair.

"I can't believe she fainted!" Sebastian ranted. "And I can't believe I didn't! Why does that bitch get money she didn't earn? She never did a damn thing around the house! Are you *kidding* me?"

"Mr. Garrett." Ajay hissed, stoically, quietly, but with a look of contempt on his face. "You're embarrassing yourself."

"Embarrassing mys-...? Whose side are you on anyway? And since when did you call me Mr. Garret? You always call me Sebastian when we play golf!"

"Yes, of course, but I'm just doing my job today."

'Who the hell told her to come to court anyway? It was you, wasn't it? You son of a bitch! I trusted you! And you let *her* have half of ours, I mean my money?"

"Mr. Garret, may I ask you a question?"

"I guess," he growled

"Do you really need all of your money?"

"I'd like to save for retire-"

"With all due respect I think you were set for retirement years ago. Don't you think you at least owe Patricia the courtesy of giving her what is rightfully hers? I'm not trying to be nosey and contrary. I'm not even trying to judge you, but there are two people in every marriage and for a marriage to function even with such fragility as yours seemed to, there needs to be two committed people. The judge, myself, Ms. Reuben, and *you* yourself know darn well that she is entitled to that money."

"Darn? Are we a boy scout today, *Ajay*? See? I'm still calling you by your first name."

"That's Mr. Vindhu to you, sir. I wish you luck, Mr. Garrett, but if you think you are going to make me change my mind in regards to this afternoon's outcome, you are mistaken. Have a nice evening." And with that, he walked down the hall through the double doors, and out of the courthouse, leaving Sebastian slack-jawed in his dust.

Patricia got out of the building before she had to face Sebastian because she wasn't sure how long this feeling of euphoria was going to last and she didn't want to risk losing it by having another encounter with him.

Because she'd refused to hire her own lawyer the court had appointed her one. She was fresh out of law school, timid and said very little. If it were any other case she would have lost her pants but since the vast majority of the room knew Sebastian pretty well it was an easy win on her part regardless of the inexperience of her attorney. And because the court also knew Patricia there was no bias whatsoever.

Now, what to do with the money? My goodness, what a terrible problem to have, she giggled to herself. The only person she wanted to tell her amazing news to was away on a silent retreat with her fellow yoga instructors until Sunday. She got home and as Poppy greeted her at the door she squealed "We're rich, girl! We won big time!" The dog barked in response, dancing excitedly around the kitchen. There was no better individual to share her news with.

Chapter Fourteen

Melody

Dr. Gamal continued to visit Estelle, twice a week on Wednesday and Friday mornings. She was very diligent and reported back to Melody after each visit. Unfortunately, with the exception of Estelle "training" Poppy that afternoon in the middle of the thunderstorm, there had been little to no change. Meanwhile Melody and Flynn met with Dr. McIntyre twice a week, sometimes with Estelle and sometimes in his office, privately. Melody felt like she was beginning to let go of a lot of the hurt and anger she had felt towards her mother. She wondered, however, if Estelle's continued despondency might be due to her hearing the therapy conversations.. Melody knew her mother wasn't a fool and understood that she had fallen short as a mother many times. Melody also knew that she had fallen short as a daughter. However, though Flynn had urged her to do so, Melody had yet to formally apologize to her mother, or even admit to the fact that she was nearly absent in her father's final days and had hardly spoken to her mother since his funeral. Yet, Melody, in her impatience and she hated to admit foolishness, was getting frustrated with her mother as she seemed to be allowing herself to deteriorate.

Flynn was working late one evening, so Melody visited her mother alone, and spoke to the nurses about her progress. She was supposed to have a physical therapist visit her once a week for an hour, not to bring her to the rehab gym, but just to work with her on some basic mobility retraining, such as lifting her legs, holding a spoon, a pen, etc. She had come to show her mother support but more so to see if today's session had gone well. She very well could have called the front desk, but she was a firm believer that in-person conversations are more productive, and besides, she was suffering a bit of PTSD making phone calls ever since the day the grocery store called her and told her that her mother had lost her way.

"Good evening, Mrs. Malley, how are you tonight?" The head nurse, Abigail asked.

"I'm fine thank you. I was just coming to ask about Mom's progress this afternoon with physical and occupational therapy, and to visit her of course."

"Mrs. Malley, I'm not going to lie. And I'm probably not being impartial either so please keep this conversation between you and me."

"Of course."

"I think your mother can do more than she lets on. I don't think she's trying. I think she has the physical strength and endurance in the very least to attempt the simple tasks asked of her and at the most go down to the gym and attempt to stand on her own. I'm not a psychologist at all, but I think her unwillingness is not physical but mental. It's just my opinion, Mrs. Malley."

"Thank you for your opinion. I think I agree with you." And with that she went into her mother's room. She didn't mean to unleash hell's fury on her but that's what she ended up doing.

"Hi, Mom." No response. *Of course not.* "Mom, I spoke with the head nurse just now." Melody swore she saw her mother lower her head even further but she couldn't prove it. "She told me she doesn't think you're trying. I believe her. I think you have more in you then you're letting on. I think you know what's going on. You were very cognitively aware during our conversations with Dr. McIntyre and I think some of the things we said hurt you. But Mom, a lot of things you did hurt me. A lot of things you didn't do hurt me. I guess I'm kind of bitter. I don't want to be, but the truth is, it wasn't my job to make you like me. I was a child and as I became an adult I was still *your* child. I still don't know what you want from me but I know what I want from *you*. I want you to get better. I want you to stop fucking around with our heads and try. You spent your whole life fighting for others, for animals and people so you can't tell me that you're going to give up on yourself. That's bullshit. If Dad were here he'd be pissed. He would know you can do better too. He was your biggest fan. No, he was your second biggest. I was your biggest. I'm not sure if you were ever my biggest fan but I was yours. And that's kind of backwards since you hardly looked at me half the time, but in spite of the fact that you didn't do much as my mother, you truly were my inspiration. Mom, please try. Please don't give up." And with that, she left her room, and headed home.

Love is a complicated thing between family members. We want to be everything to everyone and want to make our parents proud. Melody had spent the majority of her life walking the fine line of pleasing her mother and becoming a person she can live with. She felt that she had somehow failed at both and that if not for her father and husband her sanity would be on the fringes. However she knew that it was not up to either of them to make her feel complete and validated. This was her job and for the life of her she didn't know where to begin in this endeavor.

It was Wednesday at noon and her boss walked over to the front desk. "Hi, Melody, Megan called in sick this afternoon and was scheduled to lead story time. Would you be willing to do it? It's only an hour. We can cover the front desk for you."

"Sure!" she replied. She'd never been asked to lead story time before, though it was something she would have loved to do on a regular basis, rather than working at the front desk checking out books and pointing people to the "adult" section. In between organizing books to be shelved and checking out the occasional patron, Melody glanced down at the book Megan was going to read this afternoon. *If You Give a Mouse a Cookie.* She sighed. She wasn't particularly inspired by this book, and it took all but two minutes to read and she had no idea what she was going to do the other forty three minutes as an activity. She wandered into the craft room and found the dye cut machine with images. She found one of a mouse and one of a slice of cheese but no cookies. That was easy, she could draw cookies. She found some sequins and the smallest of the colorful puff balls as well as some brown construction paper and a bunch of glue sticks. She prepared the after story time craft with minimal effort. She shuddered. Was this all there was to leading story time? No wonder they had interns do it. She looked at the book and the bag of balls in her hand. She didn't even like mice or Laura Numeroff for that matter. There were so many better children's books. She wished she was reading *Stellaluna.* That was her favorite book as a child.

Fifteen story time participants were sitting cross legged on the rug adorned with a variety of children in a circle holding hands. when she sat down on the wooden stool, the book in her hand. The children ranged from age four to nine. Besides Cody poking his little brother Jamieson in the head and Jamieson whining "stoppppp" and their mother shushing them from a few feet away the crowd was quiet. Little Hannah, who apparently had a huge affinity for *If You Give a Mouse a Cookie* as she colored its cover red, was sitting in the front row, cross legged, expectant.

She picked up the book, took a deep breath, and began to read the first line when suddenly she stopped. She put the book down, looked at the kids and said "If it's ok with you guys, I'm going to tell you a story today instead. I'm sure Ms. Megan will read *If You give a Mouse a Cookie* next week but today we are going to do something different." The crowd responded with silence. She continued.

"Once upon a time there was a dog. This dog did not have a home. She didn't have a dog mom or dog dad. She was hungry a lot but she was very smart so she found food once in a while. Because she lived in Denver she drank snow as water. She just made sure it wasn't yellow snow!" The kids giggled. "Living alone was scary when you were a puppy, especially when it got dark and cold. One day she wandered into a very busy place. There were lots of people running around everywhere and driving these big scary cars. The little dog felt very lost among all these people until she found one person, a lady who fed her some treats. The lady didn't want a dog as she'd never had one before. She had no idea how to take care of one. But the dog wouldn't go away and she didn't want to leave her on her own again so she took her home.

"This lady lived with a man who was not nice. He said NO DOGS!" The kids gasped and shrank back at the last two words. "So she left and took the dog to live with a friend. For the first time in a very long time the lady felt happy and the dog felt happy too. This dog loved to eat and her favorite thing to eat was popcorn. So the lady named her Poppy! She was not going to keep her at first, but her friend told her she definitely should and her friend was very smart so she listened to her.

"The lady knew the dog was very special. So special in fact that she got her a job! A job in a place called a nursing home where old people lived who were sick or needed care. A lot of these people were sad, and Poppy and the lady walked around cheering them up. There was one lady who lived there who was very sad and had not spoken in a very long time. But Poppy, the dog who was lost and was now home, knew that in some way, in a way that only a dog can, she was going to help this lady find her way again, just like her new mom had led her home."

She paused and looked at the kids. Everyone, even Cody was sitting still, and thirty eyes were all staring at her. She looked up at the parents and caregivers who had brought their children to story time today. They were staring too. She continued. "And the moral of the story is…." she paused. "The moral is that the most unlikely of creatures can do the most amazing things. Never think you can't do something big. You certainly can." She looked at the clock and realized that the story had taken eight minutes to tell. She had thirty seven more minutes until story time was over and the only craft she had prepared involved cookies. She began to panic until one child after the next raised their hands.

"Is Poppy real?" Ginny asked.

"Yes, she is." Melody smiled. "I have met her."

"I have a dog!" Avery exclaimed. It wasn't really a question but Melody smiled as she was the youngest participant at four years old. Her mother reminded her to raise her hand next time.

"Where did the lady find Poppy?" Celia asked.

"At Walmart!" Melody replied.

"Man, I hope we find a dog at Walmart one day." Celia exclaimed.

"How do dogs learn how to work at nursing homes?" Gabe asked.

"Excellent question. If you stick around after the story time I can tell you a little bit more about it."

After she dismissed story time she was flocked by ten children of various ages as well as their parents and caregivers asking questions. She glanced nervously at the front desk hoping that Alexis didn't have too many customers lined up, or she'd have to excuse herself and go help. So far there was only one person in line.

"Do you know how you can get dogs in this program? Our dog Harry is the sweetest!" Avery's mom, who enjoyed talking as much as Avery, asked.

She felt a tug on her shirt. She looked down at Hannah. "I like the mouse book but I like this story too. I wish I had a dog." Melody smiled. "Dogs are great. They may ask you for a cookie sometimes too." Hannah giggled and ran off to her mom. After the slew of questions were answered to the best of her ability she went back to the front desk and began organizing books to be reshelved when Julie, Cody, and Jamieson's mom came to the front desk with a stack of books, many of them Clifford stories. The boys had run off to the door and as usual Julie seemed rushed but she took a moment to thank Melody for the story. "Jamieson is obsessed with story time but it's harder to engage Cody. He's my more, uh, spirited child! He really seemed to enjoy the story today and requested all the Clifford books! Thank you for a story time both my boys enjoyed. I have to go before they run out the door, but I do hope you get to tell more stories. My kids really enjoyed it! Thanks again! Bye!' And she walked quickly off to get the boys.

As she walked in the door, Flynn was in the kitchen getting some chicken out of the refrigerator. "Hi love, how was work? Chicken alfredo tonight?"

"Sounds delicious and actually work was very interesting today."

"Do tell."

The girl who does story time called in and Andrea asked me to fill in." She rolled her eyes. "I guess it was between me and Alexis and we both know Alexis isn't a fan of kids so maybe she was desperate and chose me. Anyway, the book she was going to read was *If You Give a Mouse a Cookie*. It's a nice book but it literally takes two minutes to read and I had no idea what I was going to do the rest of the time. So I threw together this art project with brown construction paper and sequins for the chocolate chip cookies, and I knew it was silly even as I was putting it together. I actually started to get nervous, but at the last minute, right before I was about to read the book I took a different avenue. I began telling the story of Mom and Poppy. I kept it simple by talking about how Patricia rescued Poppy and she saw that she was special and thought she could train her to be a helper dog. She went into a nursing home and helped the people there, and I touched a little on Mom, and how she has been helping her. The kids *loved* it. They began asking a lot of questions about what a service dog was and even the parents were asking how to go about getting a dog certified to visit the sick. It was really great actually. Even the kids who normally don't listen seemed really intrigued."

"Amazing,"

"What is?"

"Your Mam is tucked away in a nursing home, and somehow, through you she is still bringing awareness about animals."

"You're right."

"You and mam aren't as different as you both think. I saw that the moment I met her."

"You did, did you?"

"Yes, I see things."

"As long as you don't see dead people! Ok, let's get cooking. I skipped lunch today."

She was reaching for the heavy cream when he phone buzzed. She put the cream on the counter and opened her phone. It was Dr. Gamal. She let it go to voicemail. Once the sauce was simmering and the pasta was boiling she listened to the message.

"Hi, Melody. I attempted to call Flynn earlier and it went to voicemail. I've actually been trying to reach you both all day. I have some news about your mother. Don't worry, it's promising news. If you could both meet me on Friday in the afternoon sometime, I need to talk to you. This information could change the trajectory of her care and even speed the healing process. Of course I will explain in more detail in person. Please give me a call back so we can schedule a time."

Flynn came walking in with his phone. "Oh crap, my phone was charging in the bedroom. I guess I didn't hear it go off before. What did her message say?"

Melody replayed it and he listened intently, smiling at the end. "That's really wonderful news, Mel. I know Mam is a fighter. Now all we need to do is remind her of that. She's fought for others, now it is time for her to fight for herself.

"Mr. and Mrs. Malley, thank you for meeting with me. I have met with your mother a few times as well as going over her charts. I have good news and bad news. I will give the bad news first. Your mother seems to be in what we call a catatonic state. What this basically means is that she is in a state of shock. Her efforts fail in comparison to her abilities. From here I am going to segue into the good news, which is that it appears that your mother does not have Alzheimer's disease."

"Oh, that's amazing. I am so glad we got a second opinion." Melody sighed with relief.

The doctor nodded. "It is good news indeed. What the CT scans showed, and this is what we are solely relying on right now, since Mrs. Clayton's behavior is not indicative of her true state. The scan showed a series of small strokes which had led to some dementia-like symptoms. Pair that with the fact that at the time of her decline she was suffering from depression and as a result, malnourishment, this is likely what caused some of the incidents that you were informed of before her placement in Sunshine Estates. At this point, skilled nursing care is the best route as she is obviously quite incapacitated, however as time goes by, and hopefully the catatonia fades, she should find the will to seek rehabilitation. Your mother's healing relies on her desire to heal. I would absolutely recommend more pet therapy for her. The resident cat seems to have taken a liking to her and it seems you have become friendly with the woman who brings the dog by. I have a dog myself and believe animals play a vital role in healing, both physically and emotionally."

"I totally agree." Melody replied, unsure of what else to say as Dr. Gamal had shared quite a bit of information.

As usual, Flynn took over with the questions. "Dr. Gamal I know you did not know Estelle before now, so you don't know what kind of person she was. She was extremely determined and would always stand up for what was right. She had a huge heart and she was a very proud woman. She lost her husband a little over a year ago and we know that was very hard on her. Unfortunately, Melody and I were a bit lax in supporting her. We have our reasons but reasons aren't excuses. I believe that you are right. One thing led to another.

The depression led to the malnourishment, which may or may not have led to the mini strokes but regardless, the catatonia makes sense. I believe she was in a state of shock, as she has always been extremely independent and any glitch in that would have caused significant distress."

Dr. Gamal nodded. "Absolutely. Different people handle things differently, and I believe her catatonia could be the result of many things. Shame over her unusual behavior definitely could have been a factor."

As they walked to the car after their appointment with Dr. Gamal they were both quiet, wondering how Estelle was going to recover. They knew she had the will but at the same time she had deteriorated so rapidly, that this alone could have been enough to cause her permanent damage. But it was good news that she did not have Alzheimer's. Melody began to feel angry at Dr. Anders all over again for his misdiagnosis and his general lackadaisical attitude towards their whole family. But she didn't have time for that now, she needed to contact Patricia and see if she could visit her mother as much as possible. After all, if Poppy's story could intrigue a group of elementary school kids, surely it could inspire others as well.

Chapter Fifteen

Peach

Her phone rang as she got home from her yoga class. She took a swig of water as Poppy raced over to greet her. She petted her and looked at the phone. It was Melody. She sent her a text saying, *"Hi, just got back from yoga, will call you after I shower!"* She received a thumbs up emoji in return.

After a shower she called Melody back.

"Hello Melody, how are you? How is your mom?"

"That's what I wanted to talk to you about. My husband and I just came back from speaking with her doctor. Her new doctor, who I may add, actually seems to *care* about her and her progress. It turns out that after further testing that my mother doesn't have Alzheimer's after all."

"Oh, Melody, you must be so relieved."

"Definitely. But even though it's not Alzheimer's, mom's condition is serious. She seems to be in a catatonic state as a result of shock over such a rapid decline. You didn't know Mom before her illness but she was quite a force to be reckoned with. I guess I always wished I was more like her. But now, I do need to be more like her because for the first time in her life she is going to need someone to stand up for her. And the person she needs me to stand up against, oddly, is herself."

Peach nodded then felt stupid because they were talking on the phone. "Listen, Melody, I have to go to go to my ex-husband's lawyers office before it closes to sign some papers. Can we meet tomorrow or Sunday to discuss this further? I really want to help you help your mom. She has grown quite dear to me as well as Poppy."

The two ladies met at Starbucks on Speer Blvd on Sunday afternoon.

"Hi, Melody, thank you so much for meeting me. I actually wanted to share some news with you as well."

"Great, what's your news?"

"My husband and I recently divorced." She laughed. "That's definitely the good news, but there's more. His lawyer encouraged me to show up in court, though initially I had no desire to do so. All I wanted was it all to be done and over with, as I want to move on with my life. Well, now the fact is that I can move on with my life as a half millionaire! I received half of his fortune." Melody's already pale skin grew more so, though she wasn't sure why as this wasn't her win, or her ex, or her money. She had realized that in the past six plus months she had grown very fond of this woman and her miracle dog. While mom's progress wasn't obvious to everyone, she knew that something in her lit up when Poppy came to visit. She was extremely happy for Peach.

"That's really amazing. Any idea what you are going to do with it?"

"You know, I could do what I always wanted to, move to Boulder and live in this upscale cabin, and write and craft and do yoga but now that sounds selfish. I might very well move to Boulder but beyond that I don't know what I want to do. I feel like I need to make this money count. All those years I was married to Sebastian we just hid our money away, and we never shared a penny. He bitched every year when we had to pay taxes though we always ended up with more than enough. He forbade me to give a cent to charity, and when I gave any of my own personal earnings to a charity he would yell at me for hours. Sometimes I'd wish he would just hit me or something and be done with it, but he would yell. And yell and yell. I think I want to use this money, all of it, in spite of him. I want his fortune to go where he never wanted it to go. To help others in need. I just don't know where yet."

Melody sighed. "I wish there was a way that more people could be visited by therapy dogs if they need it. In some ways we are fortunate because Sunshine Estates is a very nice nursing home and has a program like that. Some hospitals have programs too. I think it's such a wonderful idea though I still wish my mother would make more of an effort to get well." Melody paused as she heard herself.

"I wish you would make more of an effort to make some friends. To find a boyfriend. To get a better job. To apply yourself. To be less shy." Melody's mother's words reverberated inside her head.

"Melody? Are you ok?" Peach looked at her, concerned.

"I'm fine. It's just the exact same thing my mother always said to me when I was growing up. 'I wish you would make more of an effort.' And now the tables have turned. Only this time I'm the one telling her to try harder, because her doing so determines the rest of her life."

Peach smiled. "Melody, do you hear yourself?"

"Yes I do. I've been a shit daughter."

"Why do you say that?"

"You probably don't want to know."

"Every family has mishegas."

Melody laughed out loud. "How do you know that word?"

"Jewish girl, born and bred!"

"Same! Mom is Jewish. Dad wasn't but he embraced Judaism, though he never officially converted. I miss him…."

Peach smiled. "I bet. I'm sorry I don't know what else to say. Fortunately, both of my parents are still alive. I know your father would be proud of you…."

"Dad would be pissed." Melody stated.

"Why do you think that?" Peach asked.

"He wanted me to take care of her," Melody replied, determined not to break down at Starbucks. "But I haven't. My husband has wanted to but I've held him hostage. Do you know we went to Ireland to visit his family right after dad was diagnosed with cancer? I didn't even tell him until after we returned and he was so mad. Looking back I don't blame him. I've convinced the both of us that Mom is strong and she'll be fine. But Dad was her life. I know she loves me but if I thought she enjoyed being a mother—I was fooling myself. I've always resented that and I was always as they say 'Daddy's girl'. By default really, since my mother wouldn't give me the time of day. Dad was amazing though. He taught me so much. This hot mess here is only half of who I am, because at least I had a loving and encouraging father."

"You are not a hot mess. Not in the least. You are a caring and courageous person who was going through a lot of emotions when your father got sick. We all make decisions and lie to ourselves to justify our behavior. I spent half my life lying to myself that there was good reason to stay married to a man who treated me like garbage. There was no reason. I could have left him years ago but there was a part of me that was afraid and I let that part of me make my decisions. I lost so much. My passions, my identity, even my nickname. He refused to let me go by Peach because he thought it was stupid so I refrained from using it."

"That's so awful." Melody replied. She was unable to relate to having an abusive husband just as Peach was unable to relate to having a deceased parent. She counted herself blessed that she'd married a person that would support her no matter what and had for their whole marriage.

"My parents' marriage was a model for me growing up. Mom might not have been mom of the year by any means but she and Dad loved each other passionately. I truly found someone like my father, loving, dedicated and supportive.

Peach nodded. "You're really blessed. Like my mother always says, everyone has some *mishegas*, and like Rosanne Rosannadana always said 'It's always something!'"

Melody and Flynn continued to have frequent meetings with Dr. McIntyre and her mother as well as meetings with Dr. Gamal. The meetings with Dr. McIntyre were frustrating, as she felt like she had said everything that needed to be said, and the ones with Dr. Gamal were disheartening because it seemed like mom's progress was at a standstill.

"That felt totally pointless." Melody complained to Flynn as they walked to the parking lot, after their most recent session with her mother and Dr. McIntyre. "Like we are repeating the same conversation and getting nowhere.

"I totally agree." Flynn replied. "Hey, did it ever occur to you to write a poem to Mam?"

"Mom hated my poetry when I was a kid. And besides I haven't written in years. I think I stopped when Dad got sick and have not picked up a pen since."

"I understand but I don't think it could hurt either. I mean Mam isn't exactly Mam these days anyway. I, for one, love your poetry.

And even if you don't want to show it to her, maybe writing a poem would be cathartic?"

She nodded. "Couldn't hurt."

Chapter Sixteen

Melody

Melody was proficient in every form of documentation on the computer, Google Docs, Microsoft Word, Excel, etc. But there was one form of writing which she preferred for writing personal pieces. A pen and paper. That night after getting ready for bed she sat down at her desk and did just that. She took a deep breath and conjured every muse that ever existed in hopes of writing a decent poem to illustrate a fraction of what she had been feeling.

Somebody
I have never felt like somebody
In front of you
I have always felt like a performer
Doing an impossible feat
Leaving me exhausted
And unseen
I am tired and now
You see nobody
Hear nobody
Acknowledge nobody
And the only upside is that
Maybe, now
The rest of the world
Understands a fraction
Of what I have lived
Experienced
Since the very first day
I was born.

She read and reread the poem and took a deep breath. Every word was true. She took a moment to mourn that fact, and showed it to Flynn who also took a moment to mourn with her. Melody wasn't sure what was worse. The past forty-five years or the past eight months. She missed her dad. She needed his wisdom.

That night she dreamt. She dreamt that Mom was lucid and she invited her to have coffee and talk with her. She waited and waited until it was obvious that she wasn't going to show up. She got up to leave and saw a familiar figure walking towards her. It was her father. She did a double take, looked again to make sure it was really him, and ran to him, like she did when she was little, right there in the coffee shop. In the dream he was an old and frail version of himself, so she stopped running and gently embraced him. Feeling tears in her eyes she motioned for him to come outside with her. He followed her and they both leaned against her car and she wept into his arms for what felt like forever. Finally, she looked up. He nodded at her knowingly, like he had so many times in the past, but this time he couldn't possibly know why she had been crying. So she explained. When she was a child, a teenager, and finally an adult she had a habit of speaking very quickly and sporadically when she was excited or upset and her father had the uncanny ability to understand her anyway. The dream was no exception.

"Mom was supposed to come. I wanted her to meet me here so she could speak to me and listen so I could tell her how I am feeling and apologize to her for not being there when you were sick and later when you passed away. I've been a horrible daughter, but she has been a horrible mother. She couldn't even be bothered to show up today, so now she'll never know how I feel. I'm *definitely* not giving her a second chance." No matter how old Melody was, she was always a child in her father's arms.

Stuart looked at his daughter. "Mel. My Shira." He always called her Shira, her Hebrew name which means "song" as her English name is Melody. "You cannot expect anything from Mom. I don't doubt she loves you very much. But she won't change. People don't change. Estelle will always be Estelle. I will always love her, but I cannot expect her to be anyone else. You cannot either. I know she has disappointed you time and time again as you were growing up, and I am so sorry. We both love you so much, but some people are natural parents and some are not. Your mom has a different kind of spirit. She always will. All you can do is love her and accept her all the while protecting your own heart. It's a balance. There were so many times in our marriage that I had to bite my tongue, hold my breath and just accept her. There were times when I did not. There were things she had to accept about me also." He smiled then. "I suppose the ways I fell short of her expectations made up for some of the ways she didn't meet mine. We were even. But we still love each other. Let Mom surprise you. But don't go around expecting her to change. She has the same amount of intention of changing as you do. None. But I love you, Shira, exactly as you are. You are my song, every note perfect. Go live your life and embrace who you are. There are people on earth and beyond who are crazy about you. Never forget that and don't forget to be your own biggest fan. You owe that to yourself."

She woke then and for the first time since he passed away, the longing ache for her father had subsided, if just a bit. She clenched her fist, holding onto his words like a treasure. This evening there was to be another session with Mom, herself, Flynn and Dr. McIntyre. She was ready.

When Melody and Flynn walked into room 112, Dr. McIntyre was already there. He was smiling. The old gray cat was sitting next to him and he was scratching his head. Melody smiled inwardly. Her mom needed animal lovers on her side. Still as anxious as she was for Mom to recover, she had plenty she needed to say. Her mother was sitting up, and not smiling exactly but she was looking up and she didn't have the same look of despondency on her face as she had for practically the whole of the past year.

"Mrs. Clayton had a good day." Dr. McIntyre greeted them. "She did well in physical therapy today and ate a little dinner. It turns out she's more a fan of salad than the meat heavy fare they've been serving her."

Melody almost smacked her forehead. *Duh, we could have told them that.* Neither she nor Flynn had realized that she had meal options. Not that it would have mattered much in the beginning, but maybe these past few weeks, she would have eaten more if it were the food she preferred. Mom never was a fan of meat, and she was an advocate for healthy eating, among other things. Still, though her appetite had seemed to increase, Estelle still said very little.

"Mrs. Malley, would you like to start this evening? I know your mother understands you. I know she wants to hear from you, though she may not be able to express it at the moment. She needs you, as you are, with all of your words and feelings even if it may not seem that way."

Melody took a deep breath. "Mom, I had a dream last night. In the dream, Dad was there but you weren't. In the dream you let me down and the reality is that you have let me down in the past repeatedly. There were so many times that I needed you and you were absent. It hurt and it still does. However, in the dream Dad spoke to me, and I realized something. He said that I can't change you. And he was right. I think the reason Dad loved you so much, and the reason you loved him was because he took you as you are. That's harder for a child to do, because we have certain needs that a spouse doesn't. You didn't show up and it hurt, but the truth was I don't think you could. That's not who you are, and it doesn't make me feel better at all, and I still think you could have tried, but the truth is not everyone can be a good mother. You are a good person, Mom. You care deeply about so many things and I don't doubt that you love me. I know you or Dad would give me anything to see me thrive. He could show it. You couldn't. And now we're here. And we let you down. I let you down." Her voice cracked then. "I did to you exactly what you did for me. I didn't show up for you. I didn't show up when Dad passed away, I didn't comfort you at the funeral, I didn't come to help you clean out his closets, and once everything was over, I went on with my life and to be perfectly honest with myself, I tried to forget that you existed. I lived my life as an orphan, when the reality was that my mother was very much alive and needed me desperately. I failed you and now you are here. I want you to get better. I don't care if you change, Mom. I just want you to exasperate me for many years to come." She laughed a little then. "You can be ridiculous, but I'd rather have a ridiculous mother than no mother at all. I miss Dad, but it doesn't mean that I don't love you."

Estelle

Estelle heard bits and pieces of what this lady was saying. She knew this lady. This lady was short, but pretty like her and she seemed emotional somehow. She could feel a longing for her from this woman, and she tried to understand why.

It was September 10th 1996, her and Clayton's 20th wedding anniversary. Melody was away at college and they had the house to themselves except for the three dogs and two cats. They were fostering a puppy. His name was Rocky and he was purebred beagle and purebred perfect in her eyes. He whined to go outside in the middle of the night and often forgot and peed on her carpet but she didn't care. He would snuggle in bed with her and she didn't want to give him up. She patted his silky head as he chewed on a rubber toy.

Stuart walked into the living room. "Do you know what day today is, my love?"

"Yes, Saturday which means I have the whole day to spend with this angel. My gosh, I don't want to give him up, but he needs a forever home! Stuart, isn't he adorable though?"

"He is. Melody just called. We talked for a bit. She's doing great at school, taking a lot of English courses."

"Very good."

"Estelle, today is also special for another reason."

"Oh, crap it's not her birthday is it?" Stuart closed his eyes, took a deep breath, opened them and smiled at his wife. "It's our 20th wedding anniversary."

"Oh, yes right, oh my gosh, Stuart, I love you, I do. I've just been so busy trying to find a home for little Rocky I forgot. My gosh, can you forgive me?"

"You can apologize tonight."

Estelle laughed. "Ok, let's go to your favorite restaurant. Rocky will stay home," she promised.

He couldn't help but laugh. He would not have been surprised if she'd wanted to take the damn dog with them. But looking at her and her commitment to bettering the lives of animals, made him fall in love with her all over again.

Being in the rescue world had made Estelle completely scattered and pea-brained in every other aspect of her life. She had missed her sister's wedding in LA because she was teaching a seminar on training. She had missed numerous recitals for Melody because of commitments she had made for the dogs and cats she so loved. She loved her family dearly. Estelle loved people and animals alike, but when it came to people, she had the attention span of a toddler. She couldn't help it. She loved people but her heart was for the dogs. Maybe she never should have married. But Stuart was the greatest two legged thing that ever happened to her. While motherhood wasn't for her, she never for a moment regretted having a daughter. She did regret how she treated her, and that she could not go back and fix it. Maybe she should stay hidden, in this confused little box, in this binding little chair, in this stifling little room forever, and that was what she deserved. She knew exactly who this beautiful lady with the strawberry blonde hair was sitting in front of her. Because she had her father's chin. But she felt better acknowledging her as a stranger, because all her life that was how she'd treated her.

Melody

Melody looked at her mother. Something told her deep inside that her mother recognized her. She knew at some point she would goof and call Flynn by name, uncovering her cloak of dementia. She knew Mom was feeble physically as a result of a series of mini strokes, but her brain was in there and she knew the exact reason why she refused to come out. It was maddening, but like the first forty five years of her life, she had no choice but to deal with it.

Chapter Seventeen

Poppy

When I first met my human she was different. She was timid somehow. We lived with the popcorn lady and she cried a lot and did a lot of stretching. Then I began to train her. We went to this special center with beefy bites and she taught me how to do stuff. I don't think she got to eat the beef bites like I did, unfortunately, but somehow, her confidence began to grow. Mine did too. I've never had people give me so much free food before. The more beef bites they gave me, the more confident I became. At home it was different too. The pheromones were different. After a while I stopped smelling fear. I began to smell something different and I can't put my paw on it but it's good.

Peach

Poppy's Palace had become a reality. She knew she had to do something huge with her settlement. She bought a home that a gentleman was remodeling. He was from Germany and he had quite a bit of money. He decided he wanted to move back home to live with his aging parents, and he sold his home. It was called Liebe Manor. Love. She knew it was meant to be. He was an older Jewish man and his name was Karl Lieberman. She thought back to what Andy said that night, when she brought Poppy to the Humane Society, about serendipity. She took a deep breath as she watched her chew a Kong toy filled with peanut butter. There were about 200 more of them in a huge storage box in the warehouse of the kennel area.

She still took Poppy to Sunshine Estate once a month to visit Estelle and a few of the other residents who had grown to love Poppy. Mr. Miller's wife, Anna, had passed away last month. She had a miniature poodle in one of the kennels named Agatha who would be coming with her on her next trip. She would be Mr. Miller's. She had arranged it with the staff and they okayed it. She knew it would help him cope to have a furry friend with him. Her goal was to connect with nursing facilities in the greater Denver area and hook them up with dogs to give to residents who needed them. She also made contacts with various hospitals that were willing to have a few dogs on some of the floors, such as the children's section and cancer ward. Peach was back. She was the badass bitch who got things done and took down names. And to those names she took down, she gave them a dog.

Chapter Eighteen

Estelle

Estelle had recovered. She was still weak, but she was up and at it, as she said. She acknowledged her daughter. Her recovery was long and exhausting. Each day she went around and around in her head on whether or not she deserved to recover. She knew that in some ways, she had planted herself in that wheelchair and refused to rise, to advocate for herself. She had spent over thirty years advocating for animals in need and the whole time, she had neglected to stand up for the one individual who needed her the most. Her daughter. And here she was, this brave woman, braver than she would ever be, by her side, encouraging her, sometimes distributing the tough love that was needed for her to get off her tuchus and try.

"Dad would be pissed." Melody would say when Estelle refused to do her exercises.

"Dad would be proud" she would say when Estelle was making progress.

There were days when Estelle couldn't look at her daughter, as the guilt was too deep, so as she attempted to rehabilitate, she thought of the dogs. The hundreds that were pulled from the abyss, not just from her rescue efforts, but as a result of their unshakable, resilient spirit. She had seen flea ridden souls transform into proud pets. Even the ones that perished did so with a dignity that she could never aspire to. As she put one foot in front of the other, their memories played over and over in her mind. And with that strength, she found herself once again.

She still got confused at times and needed some assistance but she was going back home. Just as Flynn took her arm and Melody took her suitcases to head out the door they ran into Peach.

She had a small carrier with a fluffy white dog in it. Poppy wasn't with her.

After exchanging hugs and greetings, Estelle asked about Poppy. "She's at the rescue. My friend's babysitting her. It turns out she doesn't get along very well with small dogs and I'm delivering this little lady to Mr. Miller today. Agatha is going to be his new friend."

"I heard his wife died," Estelle replied. "He gave Melody his phone number. I might call him. We might need each other."

"That's amazing, Estelle." Peach replied.

Estelle had found her humanity. She was still the same person she had always been. She spaced out when her daughter spoke sometimes. She would never be the reliable protective mother that Melody needed. But she was her mother and loving and caring for her gave her what she needed.

"Estelle, if your daughter can give me your address, I would like to come visit you in a few weeks. Is that ok?"

"Yes, please bring that little gray gal with you, I just love her, I'll cook her a brisket."

Melody laughed. When was the last time her mom cooked her anything?

"I'd better get this little pup to her new dad but I will see you all in a few weeks."

Suddenly Flynn sneezed. "Are you ok, babe?" Melody asked.

"Something rubbed against me." They looked down and there was Mac, saying goodbye. "Fancy that he finds the only guy allergic and gets fur on his jeans." They all laughed and pet the fat friendly tabby. "Thanks for everything, buddy. You're a good boy." He rubbed his broad head on everyone's hands and Flynn went straight to the hand sanitizer. "I'll miss the chap but not the sneezing."

Sunshine Estate connected Melody and Flynn to an agency that provided in-home care to seniors. The Monday after she moved back home, Estelle met Vince, her new caregiver. He was young, black, gay, and delightful.

"Hi, Ms. Estelle. Girl, we're going to have fun together. But not too much, your kids are watching! Oh my GOSH! Who are these BABIES?" he asked as he saw the wall with the numerous pets she had owned and fostered over the years. "And who is that handsome devil?"

She smiled. "That's my late husband, Stuart who put up with all the crazy pets we had." Melody had a feeling mom and Vince would get along just fine.

Peach

"So I never adopted a dog from you!" Pamela exclaimed as she breezed into Peach's kitchen.

"It never occurred to me that you wanted to, seeing as you have never cared for another creature since your divorce."

Pamela laughed. "I'm long overdue, especially if the creature I care for is grateful. I think I even have one in mind."

Every dog at Poppy's Palace is welcome to stay as long as they need, even if this is for the rest of their lives. A handful of the dogs there are unadoptable but able to be handled by the professional staff at the facility and have a place to live out the rest of their lives. The rest of the dogs are a variety of breeds, ages, and sizes with different needs and abilities to fill the needs of individuals and families. The majority of those dogs are trainable to be a companion for elderly individuals and some even as support dogs providing for various physical needs of their humans. The dog that Pamela had in mind was none of those things. She was highly adoptable but very high strung, high energy and had a level of intelligence that made compatibility with a training program impossible. She was a Border Collie, Australian Shepherd mix. She loved everyone she met including other dogs. However, her level of intelligence required skill and patience. Thankfully, Pamela had plenty of patience as well as emerging skills as a dog trainer.

A few days later Pamela drove up with the dog, sparkly pink collar and all. "Her new name is Zoe. It means life and she is full of it! She's too smart for me but she's food motivated which makes training easier. I met my match and my love on the same day. She's a keeper."

Chapter Nineteen

Melody

She was sitting at the front desk trying to find *If You Give a Moose a Muffin* another hit by Laura Numeroff that the family of nine was fond of when Andrea, her supervisor, came up to her. "Melody, can I have a word with you?"

Her stomach twisted. She knew she was not one of Andrea's favorite people and an impromptu meeting with her could not be good. As she followed her into one of the conference rooms, her anxiety continued to rev up. "Have a seat."

She sat obediently and looked at Andrea expectantly, feeling not unlike a dog.

"Melody, a few weeks ago I asked you to fill in for story time. I know you had asked me in the past to be in charge of it, but we were not going to make this a full-time position because it just wouldn't make sense to do that financially. We're still not going to make it full time, and we are still going to hire interns to help out, however I have had quite a few regular patrons come up to me and tell me how much they enjoyed your story that day. It was rather unorthodox to not feature a book, however whatever story you told, something about a dog, was it? It really seemed to intrigue the kids, even a few of our toughest customers, according to some happy parents. I even had a few of the kids ask about you. That cute little Avery wants to hear another dog story." Andrea smiled. "Melody, if it's ok with you, I would like to keep you at your regular duties in *addition* to running the story program. We'd pay you a bit more of course, and still hire a seasonal intern to help out. I think people could learn from you. You have a lot of creativity, and far be it for me to deprive the children of that."

Melody didn't know what to say. Her whole life, with the exception of her father and husband, and maybe a compassionate teacher somewhere in her past, she had never had someone compliment her this way, especially over something which she was passionate about.

She wanted to tell her mother. First she texted Flynn and he responded as she had expected. Her mom still had her cell phone and whoever was over there helping her would help her answer it if she needed. She knew Vince would be with her until seven tonight. She dialed and it rang twice before he answered.

"Melody, girl! How *are* you? Your mom is in the restroom right now, can I tell her you called?"

"Sure. It's... no hurry; just something I wanted to share with her is all. How is she doing? We were going to come visit her this weekend."

"Girl, she is doing so great, getting stronger every day. I think she misses having a dog. She tells me the same stories over and over about her dogs she's had. I never get sick of them. I'll have her call you soon."

Chapter Twenty

Peach

Poppy's Palace receives a huge variety of breeds of dog that came in from various rescues in Denver as well as Boulder. Peach had formed a good relationship with Andrew, the intake person at the Denver Humane Society who had been promoted to Rescue Coordinator. He texted her to ask if she would be willing to take a young male beagle who was pretty terrified of most things. She knew that if he was not adoptable the Palace could keep him for the rest of his life, as she had staff who were skilled and compassionate with frightened animals. She had to weigh her options to a certain extent because she knew that if she accepted an unadoptable dog that would take up kennel space for one that was adoptable but she also knew that the fate of an unadoptable dog at the Humane Society would be far worse than a lifetime at a rescue. So she said yes. After texting Pamela and jokingly asking her if she wanted to take on another doggy project after she trained Zoe and receiving a laughing emoji followed by good luck she called Andrew and told him that she would come pick him up tomorrow. He said there was no need as he was headed to Boulder to visit a friend and would take the little guy personally.

At noon the next day his blue pickup pulled up with a large kennel containing a very frightened beagle. He was hard to see as he was in the very corner of the kennel, but from what she could see, he was beautiful. She spotted a handsome red collar around his neck.

"Hi Patricia, it's good to see you again. He's sedated by the way. Otherwise he'd have been howling the whole drive here. Thank you so much for agreeing to take him. I hope you find someone special who can adopt him. I think with the right family he will blossom, however shelter life will kill him. I don't know how old he is exactly but looking at his teeth I'd say young. His energy level doesn't give his age away as he is so completely still most of the time. The only thing he moves is his mouth to howl and yowl. The poor guy." Andrew sighed. "We haven't named him. We hesitate to name a dog this scared because we don't know what his fate will be, as awful as that sounds. Naming him makes him feel more like ours and…"

Peach stopped him. "I understand. Before I decided I was going to keep Poppy I was extremely hesitant to give her a name. But now that he's here, he should have a name!"

Andrew smiled and unloaded the kennel off of the truck trailer. While Peach had decided that she was done with men after Sebastian, she couldn't help but notice that Andrew had a fine physique. It doesn't hurt to look, she thought.

Once his anxiety meds wore off, the little beagle howled into the night. And into the day. He barely ate regular dog food. In desperation, she threw some kosher hotdogs into his kennel and he gobbled those up. She saw him take a few slurps of water, but she knew he couldn't live on hotdogs. He was so nervous that his stool was loose. She tried coaxing him out of his kennel but he refused. She gave him some toys though she read beagles aren't as big on toys as they are sniffing. Barbara, one of the animal behaviorists, had a great idea. She took some wadded up newspaper and sprayed it with different smells: cinnamon, salmon flavor, wet grass and as gross as it was she even rubbed one in deer poop! He wouldn't allow anyone to walk him but this sniffing enrichment was at least a way to keep him engaged in his kennel. The vet recommended more anxiety meds and as he was accepting balls of peanut butter she was able to give them to him. Unfortunately as he was not eating much else besides the occasional hotdog he would throw up the pills along with clear bile as he was mostly just consuming water.

Peach sighed. She felt like she was in over her head with some of these dogs that came to the shelter. A little over a year ago she had never had a dog. The only pet she ever had growing up was her parents' parakeet that she'd wanted nothing to do with. Now she owned one of the largest "no kill" shelters in Boulder. Of course she had hired some of the best staff and had the best volunteers who would do anything for these dogs, but she had to admit to herself that there were some she couldn't help. A tear rolled down her cheek as she empathized with the scared little beagle.

Last year at this time she herself was in survival mode. The life that surrounded her scared her and she hadn't known what step to take next. If it were not for Poppy she would still be in the same dire straits as she was back then.

She looked at her dog curled up by the fire. In a way Poppy was lucky. Before she came to her, nobody had helped her. But nobody had hurt her either, that she was aware of. With the exception of the first few minutes of her first encounter with her, Poppy had always been very trusting. Even that mess mix Australian Shepherd Pamela had adopted was making great strides. She had no idea who had hurt that beagle. Whoever they were, she wanted to throw them into the fireplace, but the truth was they were gone and he was here and he was counting on her.

Just then she got a text from Karl. "How are the dogs? I hope Lieb Manor is treating them and you well. Over here in Germany, nagged and loved by my parents, lol. Mom is making me attend Shabbat service. It's boring just like when I was a kid. But it's good to be home. Pat the pups for me."

She texted back with a smiley face and told him she was well. Then she sent him a photo of the beagle. "I'm worried about this one. He is scared and won't eat or come out of the kennel. I wish I was better with scared dogs. Mine is a ham. I've never worked with a scared animal. Nor sure how to help him."

Karl "loved" the picture and wrote back, "maybe he needs somebody special who understands him. Off to coffee with my cousin. Gute Nacht."

She sighed. Karl was right. The little dog needed someone special to help him. Poppy's Palace was a happy place for dogs awaiting a forever home, but it was still loud and smelly, and for a skittish dog with an unknown difficult past, it could be as much of a nightmare as a run-of-the mill shelter. He needed out. But where?

"How's the little guy?" Pamela asked as she walked up her front porch, Zoe in tow. Peach was amazed at the manners of this dog. Not even Poppy listened like her. "Zoe, show Aunt Peach your new trick. Pamela made a gun shape with her thumb and forefinger. "Bang." Zoe fell to the ground. She took some treats out of her pocket and opened her hand as the dog gobbled them. "I had to use BBQ kielbasa to get her to do this one. It's kind of sick but I thought it was hilarious. When you're bored and have one too many glasses of wine, that's what you do. You look up crazy dog tricks online."

Peach laughed. "Sorry I couldn't join you last night. I was frantically picking what little brain I have left on what to do about this dog. I have so many staff and they have been so helpful but I feel mostly responsible for him.``

"Have you named him yet?"

"I'm afraid to. I KNOW we're not going to euthanize. My God I can't even imagine it. However I'm worried that he will refuse to eat for so long and keep getting weaker. He's not aggressive. But when anyone tries to handle him, he's just so terrified that you can almost feel it. I sent his picture to Karl last night as he texted me to say hi. He told me that he needs someone special to help him. I agree. I think with a dog this scared the less people the merrier. Question is who would foster or adopt him? I can imagine how disheartening it would be to have a dog that is absolutely terrified of you."

"I agree with Karl. He needs to be in a home. The kennel areas are…chaotic. Zoe thrives on chaos, but he's afraid even in a quiet environment let alone this zoo. Should we isolate him from the other dogs? Is there like a shed somewhere where he can be?"

"There's actually not. Before Karl bought this place the kennel area was a stables. When he bought it, he had a horse but he sold it, and ever since he just used it for yard supplies, rakes, hoes and the like. It was really sitting idle until I bought it but unfortunately there's no other place for him with the exception of the garage, which is really stuffy, even when the door is open. I'd let him stay here but Poppy isn't a big fan of smaller dogs and I guess he meets her criteria of "smaller dogs." Peach rolled her eyes. "Really grateful, huh?" The ladies laughed and Pamela said in all seriousness, maybe if you name him you'll have some sort of epiphany of what to do about him." They looked at each other. "Karl?" They asked in unison. Both ladies laughed. "We really do think alike sometimes!" Peach exclaimed. "I think Karl is perfect."

Naming the beagle gave her renewed hope for his future. She texted Karl, though she had no idea what time it was in Germany.

"Meet your namesake." It was the same picture she sent him last night as he wasn't the easiest to get a decent picture of.

"You called him Karl? What a handsome devil. Good luck with him. I think he'll be ok. There goes that Jewish faith. Godspeed and viel Gluck.

"I never paid you for Zoe," Pamela declared. Peach put a hand up. "If it weren't for you I don't think I'd have had the courage to even establish Poppy's Palace. You owe me nothing."

"I want to help. She took out her phone and pressed her Venmo app. She typed in some digits, hit send, looked up, and smiled.

Peach looked at her phone. "Hell no, Pamela, that's too much!"

"You need it. The dogs need it. I know there are some dogs who may have to spend their lives here and that money will go to their care and boarding. I couldn't think of a better place to donate. You and all these dogs are so deserving."

Peach had a mischievous look on her face. "Well that money will put peanut butter in my Kong for a long time!" Pamela shoved her playfully. Zoe and Poppy looked up and howled right along with them.

She opened her eyes, rubbed them, opened them again, and there was Poppy with a rubber ball in her mouth. She looked at her phone. 7:13. She groaned, rolled over, and her phone buzzed. She picked it up. "Hey Peach, while we can't adopt a dog from Poppy's Palace, we would like to make a donation. If you give me your PayPal or Venmo info I can send that right over! PS Mom says hi." She smiled. That was nice of them, she thought. She was so grateful to have met Melody, Flynn, and Estelle on her journey of taking Poppy as a therapy dog to Sunshine Estates. She'd never met a woman who had inspired her like Estelle had….wait a minute! She knew it might be crazy, but she had an idea of what to do with Karl.

She texted Melody back. "Thank you, Malleys. I appreciate your donation. Melody, I know you are headed to work soon, but is there any way you can call me back this evening? I have a proposition for you."

She waited until Melody responded, "sure. Seven?" After confirming that that was a good time she got out of bed and followed Poppy into the living room for some fetch before breakfast.

Peach really wanted to meet with Melody in person, but one of the hazards of moving to Boulder was that she was now about a half hour away from Denver. Not a bad drive at all but hard to meet during the week. Melody called at exactly seven and while she answered she told her she would really like to discuss this in person. "Could we meet for coffee in Denver on Saturday afternoon?"

"Sure, is everything ok?"

"Everything is great but I feel like this would be a good thing to discuss in person. This is a weird request but could your mother be there too? Flynn, as well? If that's not possible and she's not well enough, I understand…"

There was a pause on the other line and Melody finally replied, "How about you meet at our home at noon? I'll text you the address. We can bring Mom over. She's doing good. She still gets confused sometimes, but she remembers you and she certainly remembers Poppy."

"Great, see you guys in a few days. I'm excited to share with you."

She was excited but also nervous as she was unsure of what their response would be. She knew Estelle would love a new dog, however at this point in her care and recovery, Melody and Flynn were still in charge of her decisions and care. Besides, while Flynn cared about animals he was highly allergic.

She pulled up to the Malleys' gray and green ranch style house. While no cats were on the inside, the front door sported a cat-themed welcome mat. She rang the doorbell and Melody answered. She was wearing leggings, cozy socks, and a sweatshirt most likely from the University she attended, the University of Denver.

"Hi Patricia, come in. Flynn just went to Walgreens but will be back in a few minutes. Would you like some tea?"

"No, thank you. Maybe water?"

"Sure." She went to the kitchen and filled up three glasses. Just then the front door opened.

"Hello Patricia, it's good to see you. Melody and I spent last night contemplating what you wanted to talk to us about. We took Mom to Ocean Prime last night to celebrate her recovery. She had a lovely time, and to think her journey from sickness to health began the day after Melody and I went to Ocean Prime to celebrate our 8th anniversary. And now our 9th anniversary is in a few months."

Peach smiled so glad that Estelle's progress seemed to be heading in the right direction. She decided to cut right to the chase. She took her phone out of her purse, opened the camera up to the picture of the beagle and practically put it in Melody's face. She began talking. Fast. Like she was afraid that if she didn't get each word out quickly they may not consider the proposition.

"This is Karl. He's a beagle."

No shit, she thought to herself. *I think they can see that. Pull yourself together.*

"Karl is a special case. He came from the Denver Humane Society really scared. He is at my facility now. He's...not doing well. He's not eating. He can't keep down the anxiety meds that the vet wants to give him. He's not an aggressive dog. At all. He's just terrified of people. We don't know his back story. I have wonderful staff, a competent vet, and I think I have a pretty good handle on most dogs based on this past year's experience. But he's terrified. We can keep him his whole life. But he's estimated to be about two years old. Medium sized dogs are set to live to be at least twelve though the way his life is going he may have a heart attack. Anyways..." she sighed. *Just spit it out, Peach. You can do this.*

"I thought of your mother. I know she's not physically in the place where she can care for a dog but I know how much she loves beagles...." Her heart began to jackhammer in her ears when she felt a hand on hers. She looked up. Behind her glasses, Melody's brown eyes were staring right into her blue ones,

"You helped me love myself again, Patricia." Her eyes had tears in them. "You and your dog saved our family. I don't even know if Mom would have even begun to speak again if it weren't for Poppy. You guys gave me my mother back." She pointed to Flynn. "This guy here got mad at me when I told him how much I admired you because he insists I am just as beautiful a person as you. We have both been through a lot and in the process we each gained a wonderful friend. Peach, if it's ok with Flynn I would love for Mom to meet him."

Peach threw herself against Melody in a hug and hugged Flynn as well. "Oh thank you!"

Flynn piped up. "I'm allergic to dogs. There's no point in us meeting him alone. I think we should tell Mam. I know she'll say yes. It of course also depends on how the dog responds. Though I have a feeling being out of a shelter situation may help him, not that I'm an expert. Mam isn't in a place where she can physically care for him on her own. The good news is her mobility is headed in the right direction. She receives PT a few times a week. A lot of people are in and out of her house daily. Melody and I of course, as well as Vince, her main caregiver. Others come on the weekends, usually one of two young ladies. They all seem to love dogs enough to listen to her stories about them over and over again." He paused then and smiled a tearful smile. "It's really all she has been talking about since she came home. Been showing all of the caregivers dog after dog, cat after cat. Last week I was over…" Flynn began to laugh then. "She took out a bunch of pictures and started talking about the animals. Then all of the sudden looked at me, put them back, and apologized for showing me because she remembered that I was allergic!"

Peach and Melody burst out laughing. "You never told me that!" Melody gently shoved her husband.

"I forgot, but I think, well she should meet the dog. Maybe he can help her too."

Chapter Twenty-One

Karl

I don't know any of this. I like hotdogs. They toss me a few and I take them then they make me thirsty so I drink the water. The humans keep coming near me and making these sounds, and I think they are supposed to be comforting or something but I...I don't know these people. Everything smells new and funny and everything is overwhelming. I don't know what anyone wants from me.

The next thing I know I'm in a moving box again. The motion of the road under the kennel they put me in feels comforting and for the first time in a very long time I fall into a deep sleep. I am awakened by the jolt of the moving box and the door opens. I open one eye and the human who took me in the moving box opens it. I wish I had the gift other dogs have. The one that can tell you if a human is good or not but the problem with me is I don't think I've met a nice human. The last human I trusted hurt me. It still hurts. My tummy hurts from when he didn't feed me and my heart hurts when he abandoned me in the scary place. Ever since then I didn't want anything to do with a human.

She lifted my kennel and my weight shifted to the left and then the right. She grunted under the weight of the kennel, opened a door and finally set me down. These people were here. They were quiet but they all wanted to look at me. The human who drove opened the kennel and I was damned if I was going to come out. One of the humans was different. There were six eyes on me and I think they were just being curious. But one of the humans didn't look at me. She didn't try to make eye contact which I kind of appreciated because eye contact can be scary for me. I guess the fact that she wasn't looking at me made me want to look at her. So I cocked my head but then my nose was hit with something. Beef? Gravy? I've not been able to eat a bite of that brown stuff they've been putting in my bowl. I hadn't eaten in so long the thought of food gave me cramps. But this smell was too good to ignore. I sniffed. And sniffed and sniffed. There was no way I was leaving this kennel but at least I could soak in this heady aroma.

Estelle

She'd seen them before. The scared ones. The ones "impossible" to place in homes. The ones that were too far gone. That was malarkey! They weren't too far gone, they were let down by stupid people, was all. So she did what she did. She reached out and found people who were willing. But today there was nobody who was willing except for her. She may have trouble remembering what day it is. She may have trouble remembering if she had told that story before. She may have trouble remembering which pills to take in the a.m. and which to take in the p.m. But she knew dogs. This was a beagle. She knew he was scared. She knew he would come out of the cage when he was ready. She knew it would be awhile until he was ready and she was willing to wait. She knew. She looked at these people looking at the dog. She wanted to tell them to "stop staring. It's probably freaking him out" but she knew they meant well. They had meant well the whole time she was ill. Humans are different from dogs. They try too hard . They are passive aggressive and whiny and there have been times when she wished most of them would go away. But she looked down at her wrinkly hands. She could feel her own human frailty to her very core. Maybe, just maybe the weakness of humanity was the catalyst to the connection between us and dogs. Maybe they need us just as much as we need them. Today she was gathered with her imperfect family and the nice lady who has Poppy waiting for a scared dog to open up to the possibility of trust.

Karl

It's dark outside. She finally went to bed. I think the younger humans are asleep too and I'm out here taking a few bites of beef. It's meatier and juicier than the dry stuff in my bowl and I can't resist it. Besides, nobody is watching me. I followed it with a few laps of water which were louder than I anticipated and I hope it didn't wake the humans. Then I remembered that I was the only one around here whose ears take up the majority of their head and I figure I was safe.

Chapter Twenty-Two

Estelle

Progress is slow. But she after almost a year silent and chair-bound, though she aches at times, she's mobile. She remembers names most of the time and has learned to laugh at her foibles. She's sure Melody is having a good laugh at her mishaps as well, though the girl has shown her a deep compassion that Estelle does not feel that she deserves. Making a comeback at 76 is not as easy as at 46, so she accepts all the help she can get.

She likes Vince and remembers his name most of the time. She had never met anyone so loud yet so helpful before. She's pretty sure he's gay. He has a little girl who Estelle thinks is just the cutest. She's teaching the girl all about dogs when Vince brings her to work. She's such a polite little girl and sweetly corrects her when she accidentally calls her Melody. She doesn't look like Melody at age six, but she likes to read just as much as her daughter did. She feels a motherly connection with her, but that might be because she goes home at the end of the day, and as always Estelle is left with the dog, as well as the night nurse or her daughter or Flynn. Whoever can come that night.

They all like the dog and Flynn dons a mask. It's very sweet of him not wanting to get the dog sick as he seems to cough quite a bit. She keeps trying to explain that it's unlikely that the dog will catch his cold but he insists on a mask. He was always very considerate in that way.

The little dog who they told her was called Karl stays in his kennel. He likes her cooking quite a bit and has put on a pound or two.

Estelle hates her doctor's visits though her doctor is a gem. The first guy they took her to had a stick up his ass, but this woman is pleasant and warm and seems interested in her dog. Still she's always hated the doctor's office.

She looks forward to veterinarian visits with Karl. Karl doesn't enjoy his vet visits but he does seem to be gaining weight. Estelle struggles to understand people and she doesn't think it's because she's had a stroke. These people seem to think it is up to them when the dog decides it's going to come around, where in reality it's the dog's decision. How can humans give such an intelligent species so little credit?

She has plenty of *tsuris* day to day. She tires easily, her *tuchus* hurt from being chair-bound for so long, and her knees ache. But one thing she's not bitter about. That the dog ignores her. Her feelings aren't hurt in the least. He will come around in his own time.

One day she is attempting a crossword puzzle. Vince had left for a moment to pick up the little girl. She is looking for a word in her shrunken lexicon knowing that she knew this word before. She feels something cold on her leg and looks down. He has come out. He looks at her quickly and looks down again. She is overjoyed but very still, so as not to frighten him. She remembers something someone said to her a long time ago, or was it not so long ago at all?

"Don't be afraid to find your way home again. It's worth it, believe me. It's worth it to be lost, and then found. It's the best feeling in the world."

He moves an inch closer and she puts her hand on his silky brown and black head. His presence was every dog she has ever known and loved. She looks down at her crossword puzzle. She knows this word. She is learning its definition anew. She writes the five letters in the boxes. Trust.

Acknowledgments

The story of Poppy would not have been possible without many people. I would first like to thank Lisa Langeneckert, Heather Henderson, Dale Shuter, Nikki Miller, Paula Klender, Casey Clark, Kasey Maier and countless other amazing shelter volunteers and staff who are the people I want to be when I grow up. If not for them, Estelle's character would not exist.

I would like to thank Debbie Manber Kupfer for her amazing dedication to editing Poppy as well as the encouragement she has given me. Poppy would not be complete without her.

Finally this story is dedicated to every shelter dog I have ever known. Poppy was a fortunate dog in the story. There have been many dogs like her that I have met who have found loving homes. Some never made it out. To those precious souls who weren't adopted, fly high, you are still loved on earth.

Jamie Glaser

About the Author

Jamie Glaser is a writer of poetry and short stories. She enjoys writing for people of all ages and has written works for adults and children alike. Several of her poems appeared in the charity anthology, *Catstruck!*

She is a volunteer for the Olivette and Brentwood Animal Protective Association, as well as Tenth Life Cat Rescue. SAVE is a charity very dear to her heart. She lives in St. Louis with her calico cat, Audrey. *Poppy* is her first published book.

Resources

Below are a list of resources relating to some of the issues that you read about in Poppy

Visiting Angels (Elder Care)

www.visitingangels.com

The Women's Safe House

twsh.org/

Stray Rescue

www.strayrescue.org

Five Acres Animal Shelter

www.fiveacresanimalshelter.org

Right at Home (In home care for seniors)

rightathome.net

StlHuggs service dog training

stlhuggs.org/service-dogs/

Made in the USA
Monee, IL
06 July 2024

61378741R00080